FRIENDLY GABLES

Friendly Gables

WRITTEN AND ILLUSTRATED BY

Hilda van Stockum

BETHLEHEM BOOKS • IGNATIUS PRESS
BATHGATE, N.D   SAN FRANCISCO

Special features © 1996 Bethlehem Books
All Rights Reserved

First printing, August 1996
Second printing, July 2000

ISBN 1-883937-19-1
Library of Congress Catalogue number: 94-85297

Cover art by Hilda van Stockum
Cover design by Davin Carlson

Bethlehem Books • Ignatius Press
10194 Garfield Street South
Bathgate, ND 58216
www.bethlehembooks.com

Printed in the United States of America

To "Miffy"
with happy memories

Contents

JOAN

PATSY

PETER

ANGELA

TIMMY

CATHERINE

FRIENDLY GABLES

ONE

Good News

IT WAS the twenty-first of March, the birthday of spring, but in Canada winter still reigned. Snow was whirling all over Quebec, all over its fields and wooded hills, all over the mute St. Lawrence River in its prison of ice.

Steadily the snow came down, covering with its pure mantle the rusty confusion of railway yards and the smoking factories of Lachine, a suburb of Montreal. It also fell silently and daintily on the houses and gardens of its residential district. One of the largest gardens belonged to Friendly Gables, the home of the Mitchells. They had lived there most of the two years since they had moved to Canada from Washington, D.C.

The snow kept falling, falling, muffling all sounds, so that cars whispered past and pedestrians moved like ghosts. In this stillness, if someone had stood at the front gate of Friendly Gables and listened carefully, he could have heard a baby wailing in Mrs. Mitchell's bedroom.

One of the twins had been put into Mrs. Mitchell's arms. The other was being powdered and pinned and bundled by the nurse. The doctor had gone; there was only a slight smell of disinfectant left in the room; the perfumes of powder and baby oil were taking over.

Mother lay back on her pillows, one newborn son firmly nestled against her. She watched the other one longingly.

"Is he almost ready, Miss Thorpe?" she asked.

"Just a minute, just a minute," answered Miss Thorpe. She was a tall, angular woman with a firm mouth. Her hands were capable and strong—too strong, thought Mother. No wonder the baby was yelling, he must be seasick, the way Miss Thorpe tossed him about.

"Don't you think he's dressed enough now?" she pleaded. "I want to see if they're alike."

"All babies are alike," mumbled Miss Thorpe through the safety pin she held between her teeth.

"Oh no, they aren't. Mine were all different," protested Mother.

"That's your imagination," said Miss Thorpe, rolling the baby in a blanket as if she were wrapping a loaf.

"Give him to me," Mother begged.

"Here you are, then." And Miss Thorpe handed her the second baby, who stopped crying at once. Mother laid the babies side by side on her lap and compared them.

They both had red, crumpled faces and lots of dark, wiry hair.

"They *are* alike, aren't they?" she said. "I'm going to call them Johnny and Jimmy, after my husband and his brother. Won't John be surprised when he hears it's twins! We wanted another boy, but we didn't dream we'd get two! That makes it even—four boys and four girls. Does he know yet?"

"The doctor said he'd phone him," answered Miss Thorpe. "I have my hands full. Twins make twice the work. "

"Yes, and I wonder—have we enough diapers and things? I've only *one* cradle . . ." A worried flush spread over Mother's face.

"Never mind, Mrs. Mitchell, they'll both fit in the one for a while, and I'd get diaper service, if I were you. It's no fun, washing for twins."

"No—you're right," agreed Mother. She glanced at the clock. "It's almost three," she said. "The children will soon be coming home from school. I'm longing to show them the babies—the girls will be delighted! Is Catherine awake yet?"

"No, sound asleep," said Miss Thorpe. "Thank goodness. I had trouble enough getting her to bed. She knew something was happening and she kept wondering what the doctor was bringing in his black bag—was it a kitty? I asked her, wouldn't she rather have a little brother or sister, but she said *no*. She seems a very determined young lady. Are they all like that?"

"Oh, you haven't met the others yet, have you?" Mother raised herself on an elbow and listened. "There's Timmy." A pleased smile warmed her face. "Do you hear him?"

"No," said the nurse, folding up some towels. "I don't hear anything." But presently she did notice a faint, clear thread of sound rising from the road below and growing louder all the time.

"Good news, Mommy!" it said. "Good news!"

"Timmy is our evangelist," explained Mother. "He always has good news, and he starts shouting at the beginning of our avenue and keeps on all the way up. Sometimes it's a good mark he got at school, or a game he has won, or a friend he's made, but it's always *good* news. I wonder what it is this time?"

"You're not thinking of letting him come up here, near the babies?" asked Miss Thorpe, horrified.

"Why not?" asked Mother calmly.

"But—he'll be full of germs," warned the nurse.

Mother looked surprised. "I've always let my children see my newborn babies and no harm ever came of it," she protested.

They heard the clomp-clomp-clomp of boots on the stairs, and then the door of the bedroom was flung open and a six-year-old little boy tramped in, snow still melting on his blond hair, his cheeks red, his hazel eyes shining. He was breathing out the frosty air and brought a fresh smell into the room.

"Good news, Mommy," he began. Then he stopped as he noticed the bundles on either side of Mother.

"Two!!" he cried. "Two *babies!* You've got *two!* They came! Two of them!"

"Yes, twins, isn't it wonderful?" Mother smiled.

"Ooooh—twins," breathed Timmy, tiptoeing nearer, a holy awe on his face. "*Real* twins. I thought they only happened in books." He touched the bundles gently with his finger. "They're rather small, though, aren't they?" he said in a worried way. "I don't think you rested enough, Mother. They don't look quite finished."

"They'll grow," Mother assured him.

"Are they girls?" asked Timmy.

"No, boys."

"Oh, goody!" Timmy sat down at the edge of the bed.

"Do you think they'll ever be big enough to play with?" he asked.

"I'm sure they will, dear—sooner than you think."

"May I hold one?" asked Timmy.

"Not yet, dear; wait till they're a little older. You might hurt them."

"But when they're older I won't want to hold them," said Timmy wisely.

Mother smiled. "What's your good news?" she asked.

"Oh, I forgot!" Timmy's face regained its radiance. "There's a new girl in our class, called Philosophy."

"Philosophy?" asked Mother. "I've never heard that name before."

"I don't call that good news," came the cool voice of the nurse suddenly. "I call that bad news." Timmy looked around, startled.

"That's Miss Thorpe, dear, my nurse," explained Mother.

"Oh! How do you do," said Timmy politely.

"Pleased to meet you," said Miss Thorpe, but she didn't smile and Timmy wondered whether she really *was*.

"Well, tell me more about Philosophy," asked Mother.

Timmy heaved a sigh. "She is pretty," he said.

"She'd better be, with that name," said Miss Thorpe.

There was a ring at the door, and Timmy clattered out of the room to answer it, his loose shoelaces tick-ticking on the floor. A little later the door opened again to admit what seemed at first a basket of flowers on legs. Then the basket tumbled on the bed, giving Mother's big toe a jolt, and from behind it emerged a breathless Timmy, waving an envelope.

"Here," he said. "This says who sent it."

The nurse took the flowers and put them on the table by the window. She clucked her tongue in admiration. "Such lovely yellow tulips," she said with a sigh. "They go so well with the pink hyacinths. You'd think spring was here already." And she sighed again, for she came from England, and there the fields are green in March, and little white lambs gambol over the first primroses. Miss Thorpe found the long Canadian winters hard to bear.

Mother had been reading the note. "They're from my husband—isn't it *extravagant!*" she cried, flushing happily. "He says he'll come home as soon as his meeting is over."

"Yes, and you should be taking a nap, Mrs. Mitchell," warned Miss Thorpe. "You know what the doctor said."

"But the other children haven't seen the babies yet," murmured Mother. Her eyes were falling shut. She *was* sleepy.

The nurse chased Timmy out of the room and lowered the shades. Then she settled herself in an easy chair with a book. Soon there was only the sound of breathing and the whirring of the electric clock in the room. Mother and babies were fast asleep.

Timmy felt very important. None of the others knew about the twins. He would have to tell them. Their schools got out much later than his. He put on his ski jacket and boots again and stood outside. The snow was still falling in feathery flakes. Timmy saw Mrs. Garneau pass. She was an aristocratic French lady who lived in the brick mansion opposite Friendly Gables.

"We've twins!" he shouted.

The lady stopped. "*Comment?*" she asked.

Timmy searched for the right French word. "*Deux bébés,*" he said, holding up two fingers.

"*Tiens!*" Madame Garneau didn't look happy. Already there were too many young Mitchells so far as she was concerned. Two more seemed an imposition. How much extra noise would that make? She hurried into her house.

Timmy waited. He looked longingly down the avenue, where trees marched one after the other, wearing jaunty caps of snow. In the distance he could see the gray streak of the St. Lawrence River, still in its prison of ice.

He could hear the streetcar singing along the wires, coming closer and closer. Now the others would soon be here. Timmy ran to meet the streetcar, the loose straps of his galoshes flapping about his ankles. "Good news," he shouted, "good news!"

He wasn't watching where he was going and ran full tilt into a thick overcoat. Thus abruptly stopped, he looked up into the laughing face of the mailman, who asked, "Ai, ai, where hare you going?" in a strong French accent. "And what is thees good news, *hein?*"

"We've *twins!*" crowed Timmy. "Just born! Boys!"

He felt he was making a tremendous contribution to the world in general by spreading this stupendous piece of information before even the papers got hold of it. The mailman was duly impressed, and went on his round, delivering letters and papers and telling everyone he saw, "Did you 'ear, the Meetchells 'ave *twins!*"

Meanwhile Timmy had caught sight of his brother and sisters, who were descending from the streetcar.

"Joan! Patsy!" he yelled. "Angela! Peter! We've *twins—twins!* They've *come!* Two babies! Boys! Come and see!"

Mother Mitchell was in a deep, refreshing sleep. She

was dreaming that she was a child again, playing in the meadow. But as she picked the pretty daisies, they began to glitter and twinkle in her hands. They had turned into stars . . .

Crash! Boom! Her bouquet of stars exploded in her face.

"What's that?" She sat up, trembling. Then she sank back onto her pillows with a sigh of relief. It was only the children. They came storming into the room, and to Miss Thorpe's astonished eyes they seemed an army. Children you don't know always seem more numerous than they do when you know them. Peter, a tall boy of eleven with dark, quarreling hair and lengths of bony, uncovered wrist, reached his mother first. He bent over her with an almost grown-up air of protective tenderness.

"Congratulations," he said, kissing her. "Twins. What a bargain! Two for the price of one, eh?" Mother smiled at him. But Joan was already pushing Peter away. She was a tall blond girl of fifteen.

"Oh, the *darlings*," she crooned. "Aren't they just like Catherine when she was a baby? Can I hold one, Mommy? Let me have one, may I?" Lifting one of the twins from his reluctant mother's arms she sat down in the easy chair with him. He started to cry, but she put him over her shoulder and patted him in an expert way, to the admiration of Timmy and Angela, who were hanging about her chair. Peter and Patsy were leaning over their mother, admiring the other twin.

Mother was sitting up in bed, flushed, with shining eyes. "Aren't they *wonderful?*" she kept saying.

Miss Thorpe disapproved of the congestion in the bedroom and frowned at her.

"Oh!" said Mother. "You haven't met Miss Thorpe, who is kindly helping us out till I'm stronger."

The children suddenly sobered and turned their faces toward this unknown person. They had been only vaguely conscious of someone in the background while they admired the babies. Miss Thorpe looked formidable to them in the icy white of her starched linen uniform. Her dark eyebrows met over her nose, and her lips were pinched together. After a momentary hush Patsy got up to shake hands with her and Angela and Peter followed her example. Joan smiled from her chair, as she was holding the baby.

Miss Thorpe was clearing her throat to greet the children when a wail from the next room interrupted her. Catherine had waked up. There was a thud as she rolled out of her crib, then the sound of bare feet pattering on the floor. The door of Mother's bedroom was pushed open and Catherine entered, the wrinkles of her pillow still showing on her soft, pink cheek and her eyes dark and dewy under the pale wisps of her ruffled curls.

"Mommy!" she cried. She was clad only in a vest and panties and her fat tummy peeped through the gap.

Miss Thorpe clucked in distress. "Come, dear, let me dress you."

But Catherine avoided her outstretched hands and steered a straight course to Mother's bed.

"Look at the babies!" cried Timmy.

Catherine's eyes darkened ominously when she saw the small bundle in Mother's arms. Her face grew red. She threw herself on Mother's bed.

"I don't *want* babies," she wailed. "I want a *kitty*."

"Well, dear—" began Mother.

"Now, Catherine," said Miss Thorpe.

"Babies are much nicer!" cried Joan.

"I want a *kitty!*" yelled Catherine.

Miss Thorpe pursed her lips. "*Really,*" she said. "There are too many in this room. I'm afraid the children will *have* to leave."

"Yes, you're right, Nurse," Mother sighed. She allowed Miss Thorpe to push the protesting Catherine out of the room. Joan brought the baby back to his mother and smoothed her pillow.

"It's true, Mommy," she said, "you'd better rest. You've had *twins,* you know." And she herded the other children into the hall.

Miss Thorpe closed the door after her. "It was about time," she sighed. "What you need, ma'am, is a *nanny.*"

The children felt ashamed of Catherine's behavior. Fancy not wanting baby brothers! She was as bad as Mary Jane, who didn't want rice pudding. They'd call her Mary Jane, if she didn't stop howling. What would the new nurse think? What would the neighbors think? There—now the twins were crying too; Catherine had started them. Why did they cry? Because Catherine didn't want them, of course. How would *you* like not being wanted?

Catherine's sobs subsided. She still whimpered a few times that she had asked for a kitty; Mommy *knew* she wanted a kitty; but the wails coming from the bedroom impressed her. It wasn't long until she was happily munching a cooky, which she shared with Trusty, the dog.

When Father came home all was more or less peaceful—even the twins were asleep—so he and Mother could rejoice for a moment together.

TWO

Troubles

THERE is always something long-drawn-out and dreary about March, as if the glow spread by Christmas has finally faded and we're awaiting a new miracle. Everyone feels weary of plodding through snow; the storm windows have acquired a layer of dirt, and the very curtains droop despondently. But we know that spring is on the way and that the grayness is only a screen behind which she is dressing up for her appearance.

All the same, the Mitchell children felt very unsettled those last days of March. It was lovely having new brothers, of course, but they weren't much fun. Though they slept most of the time, they seemed to require an unreasonable amount of attention. Mother was barricaded away; you could hardly get near her; and the house was filled with the starched rustle of Miss Thorpe. Joan had made friends with her and was allowed frequently into Mother's room, which only made the others feel more shut out.

The first day after the babies' birth everything seemed to go wrong from the start, and the Mitchell children got into trouble one by one. It began with Joan's waking up late and hearing Miss Thorpe reprimanding Timmy for trying to sneak into Mother's room.

"Your mother had a restless night and she'd just fallen asleep when you woke her up, you bad boy," she scolded. Joan knew it was fatal to deal with Timmy that way. Timmy must never be blamed in the morning. It made him bad for the whole day. But if you praised him in the morning, he was good the whole day. Timmy was never anything by halves. So it was the fixed policy of the Mitchell family to find something to praise Timmy for the first moment they got up, and now Miss Thorpe had upset the applecart!

"Dear, dear," murmured Joan in distress. They were in for a bad day! The amount of mischief Timmy could do within twenty-four hours was incredible. She would try to see if the damage could still be undone, and, throwing her bathrobe on, she rushed into the hall on bare feet. There stood Timmy with his very worst look.

"She wouldn't let me in," he told Joan, glowering fiercely. "I wouldn't have waked Mommy. I just wanted to see the babies. But she said I was *bad*."

Joan recognized the unholy gleam in Timmy's eyes. She knew he was relishing the idea of being bad and frightening himself with his own wickedness.

"*Bad*," he repeated.

"No, not at all," Joan told him hurriedly. "It was very sweet of you to want to see the babies. Miss Thorpe did not understand. You see, she is new. She does not know you yet. She hasn't found out what a *good* boy you are. You must show her—"

But it was no use. The picture of himself as a veritable demon of wickedness had firmly established itself in Timmy's mind and he withdrew to his room, muttering ominously, "*Bad, bad, bad!*"

Joan shook her head and went back to her bedroom to see if Patsy was awake yet. But Patsy, who never used a pillow, lay hunched under the blankets like a turtle.

"Time to get up!" Joan said, slapping the turtle's back. There was only a subterranean growl for an answer. Joan picked up her toothbrush and towel and went to the bathroom, hoping to get there before the boys. As she washed she heard them wrestling and Daddy calling them to order.

"It's Timmy's fault," came Peter's voice, and then Daddy's gruff answer: "You're the oldest."

That business of being the oldest could be unfair, thought Joan to herself. When she returned to the bedroom the turtle was still dreaming away.

The older girls' bedroom was divided by an invisible but unmistakable line into two halves. In one half stood Joan's bed with neatly folded counterpane, clothes tidily arranged on a chair, shoes side by side on the floor underneath. Some photographs, neatly framed, hung on the wall—Grannie (who had died last winter), Mother, and Daddy. There were also pictures of Joan's favorite movie stars. On a white-painted dresser stood a mirror, some toilet articles, and a savings bank. There was a bookshelf with *Summer at Buckhorn, Seventeen* and *Jane Eyre* on it.

Though the savings bank looked black and uninteresting, it contained Joan's rosiest hopes. Joan had never been to a formal dance. She didn't have a formal dress. Her father and mother gave her a dress allowance which did not provide for such luxuries, so Joan had been saving the money she earned by baby-sitting or doing extra chores for Mother. She had been saving since she was fourteen and the vision of a formal had first dawned on her. It had meant a lot of self-denial, going without candy or casual treats, but she was nearing her goal. She had about twenty dollars now. Daddy had advised her to take the money to the bank, but somehow Joan found it hard to part with the physical possession of it. It seemed like a promise that she *would* go to a dance someday, even if she knew no boy yet who might invite her.

Patsy's half of the room was entirely different. Clothes lay scattered in mounds on the floor, or hung drunkenly from a chair. Books were piled underneath the bed: adventure stories, fairy tales, and knightly romances. The wall was covered with unframed pictures, cut from magazines: surrealistic landscapes, weird castles, reproductions of stained-glass windows. Her chest of drawers had the look of a disemboweled beast—most of the drawers were open, with their insides trailing out.

Joan gave the turtle on the bed another slap. "Patsy, you know you'll be late. For goodness' sake, get up!"

The turtle poked out a groggy face. "What day is it?" she asked.

"Tuesday," said Joan.

With a groan the turtle's head disappeared under the blankets. Then it popped up suddenly. "Knitting day!

And I've forgotten to do my ten rows! The new babies made me forget! Oh, why did you wake me? I was so happy!" The head disappeared again.

Joan, feeling it was up to her now, began pulling the protecting blankets away, but Patsy was already unwinding herself.

"Where are my glasses?" she asked. "What did I do with them?"

"They're in your hair," announced Joan, disentangling them with difficulty. "You must have been reading in bed again."

Poor Patsy's reading habits had weakened her eyes, and now she had to wear glasses. They were the bane of her existence. The oculist had promised her that with them she'd have normal vision for the first time in her life, but all Patsy knew was that the world was not half as beautiful as she had thought. What had looked like a red flower before now turned into an empty tomato can and a lovely distant lake had become a dingy tin roof.

"I don't like normal vision," she would grumble, but Daddy had made her wear the glasses anyway. They gave her the look of a young, ruffled owl.

A screech from Catherine made Joan rush to the next room, where she found Timmy threatening to behead Surshy, Catherine's favorite doll, a legacy from Angela. Joan tried to appeal to Timmy's better nature, but he was too far advanced on the downhill road to pay any attention to her. She had to wrest the doll from him, and he revenged himself by making the most dreadful faces, which scared Catherine into tears.

"I never *did* see such an unruly family," lamented Miss Thorpe as she came to investigate the noise.

Joan blushed with shame. "They're not always like

that—" she began, but Miss Thorpe wasn't listening. She had gone back to Mother's room, her lips firmly pinched together.

Joan did her best to rescue the honor of the family. She got breakfast for Daddy, who obviously missed Mother and roamed around the kitchen, the paper in one hand and a milk bottle in the other, vaguely looking for something to eat. She also packed school lunches and cooked porridge for the children, who came charging into the kitchen one by one. Timmy was first; he had by now become a regular highwayman and demanded, "Breakfast or your *life!*" Joan managed to soothe him with extra cream and sugar, and his interest in food kept him from thinking of anything else at the moment.

When Miss Thorpe came down to fetch Mother some breakfast she found a relatively peaceful scene, but Joan congratulated herself too soon. Timmy had finished his porridge, and the sight of Miss Thorpe reminded him that he was a desperate character. He made a grab for the sugar bowl and crammed a fistful of lumps into his mouth. Then, with cheeks bulging, he pulled Angela's curls and stalked out of the kitchen, slamming the door, satisfied with the rumpus he'd caused.

Angela's hair was always a temptation to him, as it hung like a shiny golden waterfall down her back.

"What a dreadful boy!" Miss Thorpe shuddered.

Angela, her head still smarting, piped up, "He's only showing off."

Miss Thorpe looked at the clock. "Oughtn't you all to be going to school?" she asked.

"Gracious yes, it's eight-fifteen!" gasped Joan. There was a general rush for books, lunch boxes, mittens, and coats. Patsy gave her usual wail of "Hasn't *anybody* seen . . ."

Then, there was pandemonium because Timmy had deliberately mixed up all the galoshes.

At last they were outside, in the biting wind, racing for
the streetcar. It was standing at the corner of their avenue
and Rue St. Joseph. The motorman usually waited for
them, but his patience could not be stretched too far.
Most of the Mitchell children had scrambled on board
and the conductor was just about to give the signal to
depart when Patsy came running, her open school bag
untidily under her arm, her coat unfastened. As soon as
she had jumped inside, the conductor, who had become
heartily tired of waiting, closed the doors. He didn't notice that a ball of knitting wool had bounced out of Patsy's
bag into the street.

Patsy yelled, "Wait—let me out!" but the conductor
growled, "*Trop tard!*" He was already five minutes late.
The streetcar went clacketing along the tracks, with the
little ball of red wool skipping and jumping behind it, as
it was still attached to the knitting in Patsy's bag. Now,
Patsy's knitting was an unfortunate business altogether,
as she was left-handed. The teacher was as puzzled as
her pupil when confronted with this peculiarity. And as
she taught in French, a language which Patsy had not yet
completely mastered, the result looked more like hic-
cups of wool than the beginning of a scarf. But Patsy was
under the illusion that she was improving, and the loss of
the ball of wool was therefore frustrating. It was such a
pretty red color too. Patsy tried to pull in as much of the
wool as she could. It was dirty, because salt had been
strewn over the newly fallen snow and had made a mess
of the road. The wet coils gathered at Patsy's feet and
gave off a nasty smell. People getting on and off the car
trod on them. Patsy's coat and mittens got muddier, while

she sadly watched the gaily skipping red ball receding farther and farther into the distance, until the car rounded a corner and the woolen strand, stretched beyond endurance, snapped.

Patsy hastily stuffed the salvaged scallops of wool into her knitting bag and took a seat. Everyone was looking at her, except Peter and the girls, who were blushing with embarrassment. Joan gave an irritated shudder. Why couldn't Patsy behave like everybody else?

They were entering the old French part of Lachine. It was a suburb now, but once it had been the estate of the explorer La Salle, who had tried in vain to reach China by way of the St. Lawrence River. In mockery, the people had called his estate "La Chine," and the name had stuck.

The Mitchell children went to three different schools. There was a one-room school for the first two grades, where Timmy went; it was near home and he could walk there. Peter attended a large, grim-looking boys' school in the middle of the town, and the girls went to a small convent school near the Lachine Canal.

Patsy's teacher was Sister Marie Rose. All the girls loved her because she was young and pretty. She made lessons into a game and learning a pleasure. This morning she told the children that Monsieur le Curé would celebrate his fifteenth anniversary as a priest in two weeks' time. The sisters were preparing a surprise for him. They had made a beautiful embroidered tablecloth which they were going to raffle off, to provide funds for a celebration and a suitable gift. On no account were the girls to let out this secret, but they were all asked to sell raffle tickets. The principal, Sister Elaine, was also organizing a special choir to sing for the occasion.

This announcement caused quite a bit of excitement,

and Sister Marie Rose wisely related her lessons to the project. They were all to write compositions on what they thought would be the best way to celebrate Monsieur le Curé's fête. As these had to be done in French, Patsy's effort was rather feeble. She had to look up so many words in her dictionary.

During recess the girls chatted of nothing else, and they came to their Domestic Science class with distracted minds. Domestic Science is a favorite subject with French Canadian nuns—doubtless a relic of pioneer days when a young woman, Marguerite de Bourgeois, started schools to teach little Indian girls to cook and sew. The Annual Exhibition of Handcrafts was an important event of the school year, and Sister Elaine justly prided herself on her excellent exhibits. No other school could boast such fine stitching, such snowy linen, such complicated Fair Isle knitting patterns. As for the babyish hairbands shown by some schools, they were simply not found among *her* pupils' work. That inferior sample of knitting was bypassed. Her pupils started with respectable scarves.

This morning she examined the homework of Patsy's class.

"*Pas mal*," she murmured in approval here and there. Madeleine Girard had finished her sweater and pressed it nicely. She could now start a romper for her baby brother. Gabrielle Le Masse was making a success of her gloves, and Leona Levine had cleverly turned the heel of her sock. But Patreecia . . . With a sigh Sister Elaine asked Patsy to produce her scarf. Though she was not yet completely discouraged, she did find Patsy rather difficult.

Patsy came forward as slowly as possible. She felt instinctively that the teacher would be displeased. Still, what could she do but open her bag?

"*J'avais un accident,*" she began hesitantly. "*Dans le—
tram . . .*"

Sister Elaine was a small fierce nun, with birdlike black
eyes. She gave an exclamation and jumped back two feet
when Patsy began pulling out the sodden, smelly mass of
woolen spaghetti.

"*Mon Dieu, mon Dieu!*" she shrieked. "Is it poss*ee*ble?"
She held her nose and waved Patsy back. "Go," she
moaned. "Take it away! I don't want to see it. *Un accident? Mon Dieu, c'est un catastrophe!*" As Patsy retreated,
trailing malodorous red snakes, there was a titter from
the girls around her.

Sister Elaine had got her breath back, and her black
eyes snapped with anger. She released a torrent of French
words, banishing Patsy from the inner circle of Domestic
Science and condemning her to gnash her teeth forever in
the limbo of incompetents. She pronounced sentence ruth-
lessly. Patsy was to stay after school and write a hundred
times, "I must keep my knitting clean."

But that was not the worst.

"You can throw away this mess," she said. Then, lowering her voice in an ominous manner, which made the
whole class catch its breath, she hissed, "Instead, you will
knit a *hairband!*"

THREE

More Mischief

HER punishment made Patsy late going home that day, and her one wish was to tell Mother everything. Mother would understand that it hadn't been her fault. "The conductor wouldn't stop," she'd explain. "Joan wanted me to pretend I'd forgotten my knitting, but that would have been a lie, and I didn't know the teacher'd be *so* mad—" Mother was sure to say the sort of thing that made Patsy feel better. She always did. So when Patsy arrived home she hurriedly kicked off her galoshes and ran upstairs to Mother's room, but she was intercepted by Miss Thorpe.

"No, dear, your mother can't see you at present. She has had a bad night and the doctor says she is not to have visitors."

"But I'm not a visitor—" began Patsy, astonished. "Mommy always wants to hear what's happened." Then, suddenly, she was aware of Miss Thorpe's opinion. It overshadowed her like a cloud. Patsy felt as if she wasn't Patsy any more, but some unknown, selfish child who did not love her mother. She fumbled for the banisters and retreated downstairs, to the living room, where Peter was poking at a languishing fire.

"Where are the others?" Patsy asked.

"Joan is washing Angela's hair," said Peter in a resigned voice. "Timmy wiped his hands on it after eating bread and jam. It was a mess."

"Why did he do *that?*" asked Patsy.

"Well, you know Timmy. He's on the warpath today," Peter growled, giving another vicious poke at a defunct coal.

"Is he all right now?"

"Oh, sure. He is playing outside with Catherine."

Patsy thought she'd better check up on them but something strange about Peter's attitude stopped her.

"Look at me, Pete," she said. Peter turned his face toward her and Patsy saw that it looked swollen and scratched. "Were you in a fight?" she asked.

"It's that Paul Lepine. He's always trying to get the boys to gang up against me. He's teamed up with some of the older boys and five of them lay in wait for me after school today and beat me up. I hadn't a chance." Peter spoke with difficulty, for his lips were swollen.

"That's mean!" Patsy was indignant. "Why don't you tell the teacher?" But she didn't need Peter's angry look to remind her that you couldn't do that. Tale-telling was the worst of sins.

"I just wish I could get that Paul in a fair fight," said Peter, grinding his teeth. "Boy! Would I let him have it!"

"Why don't you challenge him?" proposed Patsy.

"Oh, he wouldn't do it," said Peter, giving some more pokes to the fire, which put it out completely. "I think he's a coward. He'll try to play the same trick on me tomorrow."

"You can't let them beat you up every day," protested Patsy. "Why don't you get together a gang of your own?"

"And play Cops and Robbers!" mocked Peter. "What *fun!* No, I guess it's my wits against his; I'll have to outsmart him." He brightened a little. "Yes, that's what I'll do. One against five . . ." he mused. Then he grinned. "Thanks, Patsy, telling you has cheered me up," he said gratefully.

A commotion outside drew them both to the window. There they saw a sight which made them gasp and run out into the garden.

Timmy had done something which he knew was forbidden. He had taken a box of matches and a bag of marshmallows out of the kitchen. There was something brave and splendid in defying authority, he felt. But what use is it if there's no one to admire you? He needed Catherine.

"Come, Catherine," he said. "We're going to have fun."

Catherine was quite ready to believe it. With Timmy she always had fun. So she trotted after him and watched him build a bonfire on the snow, in a corner of the garden. Timmy had chosen a good spot, out of the wind, no dry shrubbery near. It was a beautiful fire, the kind Daddy made in the autumn, to burn leaves. The bright flames danced and the wood crackled. Timmy pricked marshmallows on a long stick and held them in the flames. They began to burn, but Timmy extinguished them before they were quite black. He ate the hot, melting goo. A lot of it stayed on his nose and cheeks. Trusty got very excited and ran around, barking for some. Catherine said she wanted one too. She was holding the empty paper bag in her hand. Timmy reached her a flaming marshmallow at the end of his stick and Catherine made a frightened movement with her arm, waving the bag. The bag caught fire, and instead of dropping it, she clutched it tightly and ran away screaming.

That's what Peter and Patsy saw from the window—little Catherine running with a flaming torch in her hand. She was too scared to drop it.

Luckily for her, Timmy was a brave boy. He ran to her and beat the flaring bag out of her hand, hurting his own. Then, seeing that her coat was smoldering, he threw her down and rolled her in the snow. When Patsy and Peter arrived on the scene, the danger was over. Catherine was unhurt; her thick clothing and leather mittens had protected her. But she was sobbing with fright. Timmy had a burned hand, which he was wrapping in his handkerchief. It was obvious that he knew he had been extremely naughty, so Peter and Patsy didn't waste words.

"You put out the fire, Peter," said Patsy. "I'll take the kids in."

She marched them into the house. Catherine was still sobbing, but Timmy held his head high. He wasn't going to snivel, he'd take his punishment like a man.

Miss Thorpe awaited them in the hall. She had watched everything from the upstairs window.

"Never have I met such children!" she said. "You gave your mother a terrible fright. It's your fault, Patsy, for not taking better care of the little ones. A big girl like you!"

Nobody asked me to look after them, thought Patsy, but she didn't say it. It was no use.

"Come with me, Catherine," said Miss Thorpe. "You're *filthy*. No, you can't go to the bathroom; Joan and Angela are in it." She led the child to the kitchen sink.

Catherine was protesting, "I don't like my face—"

"That can't be helped, dear," said Miss Thorpe.

Catherine took a deep breath. "I don't like my *face*—" she repeated in a louder tone.

Miss Thorpe was rubbing vigorously with a soapy cloth. "It's not so bad when it's clean," she observed, giving it an extra wipe.

Catherine made a last desperate effort. "I don't like my face *washed!*"

Timmy gave a shout of merriment, which made Miss Thorpe call him a heartless boy, laughing so soon after he had nearly burned his sister! And he'd better clean himself—he looked a disgrace.

Angela came downstairs with her hair done in curlers. She was already in pajamas and bathrobe. Joan followed, with the radiant look of a person who has been virtuous the whole day. The other children envied her.

Miss Thorpe called them into the kitchen for supper.

When Mother was around, the kitchen was the cosiest room in the house, full of lovely smells and nice things to eat. You could sit on the edge of the table or sink, and while Mother was stirring things and tasting them (and letting you lick spoons and pots) you could tell her what had happened at school and what your friends had said—and if you peeked at a new cake Mother would smile and cut you a slice and say something about the cold weather giving you an appetite. You felt happy and safe. You knew this was *your* home and *your* mother and everything was good.

But now the kitchen looked like one of those places where they send you to be inoculated against a disease. It was clean in a cold way, not friendly any more. And the smell wasn't nice, for Miss Thorpe really wasn't a cook. As they sat down at table she explained how kind it had been of her to get them their supper: it wasn't her job; she was a sick-nurse, not a cook or a nanny. But to oblige Mother she had done it this once, so the children had better behave. As Miss Thorpe spoke, it was clear that she did not expect them to behave, though they were all too depressed to be boisterous. It certainly wasn't from a desire to be troublesome that Patsy let her glasses drop into the soup; it was sheer nervousness. When she groped her way to the sink to wash them she knocked over a tumbler, smashing it on the tiled floor. The dustbin and mop weren't in their usual places, so the other children got up to help her hunt for them. When the broken pieces were finally swept up, the soup had got cold. Nobody wanted it anyway, because it didn't taste like Mother's soup. But Miss Thorpe said it had to be eaten. The children started to spoon it up reluctantly—except Timmy, who gave his plate to Trusty. Miss Thorpe called him a disobedient boy, but Timmy argued that he wasn't, because the soup was being eaten—Trusty was eating it like anything. Catherine immediately brought her plate to Trusty too, and then Miss Thorpe slapped her, which wasn't fair, for she hadn't slapped Timmy.

Catherine howled, and Daddy came in just at that moment. The children hadn't a chance to tell him anything:

Miss Thorpe did all the explaining. She made it seem as if everyone had been deliberately misbehaving from the first, and she made a big story of Patsy's negligence, as if it hadn't all been Timmy's fault really.

Daddy was shocked when he heard about the bonfire. "Didn't you know you're not allowed to take out matches?" he asked Timmy sternly.

"Yes," said Timmy, looking at his father with large, candid eyes. "But I thought to myself, I'll do it all the same."

"That was very wrong. Catherine might have been seriously burned." Daddy spoke in a sad voice.

Timmy hung his head. "I won't do it again," he promised. "As long as I remember."

Daddy's lips twitched a little. "See that you remember," he warned. Now he turned to the others. He looked grave. "I would have thought," he said, "that you older children, and especially the girls, would have understood how important it is for Mother to rest, and would have helped the nurse, who naturally has her hands full, to keep the little children out of mischief. I'm very disappointed in you."

Miss Thorpe at once leaped to Joan's defense. "It wasn't Joan's fault," she said. "She was washing Angela's hair. It was those two, Peter and Patsy, who were just lazing around while the little ones were setting each other on fire."

Here there was a cry of protest from Timmy, who said he hadn't set anyone on fire; it was an *accident*.

"Well, Patsy," said Daddy, "that means you. It isn't the first time I've noticed that your dreaming habits interfere with your duties. You let Joan take the lion's share of the work and dodge your own responsibilities. Go to your

room now, and think it over. The others can all go straight
to bed too; I'm very displeased with the lot of you. Except Joan, of course."

This was a terrible punishment, for they'd all looked
forward to their evening with Daddy and having at least
one parent to tell things to. But, though Daddy had spoken quietly, they knew he meant it. He was really angry
and they'd have to obey instantly.

The boys shared a room and were soon in their bunks.
Catherine crawled into bed with Angela while Trusty
settled himself at their feet.

But Patsy's room was empty. She could hear Joan downstairs, talking to Daddy and Miss Thorpe. Patsy's bed
hadn't been made; the empty turtle shell of the morning
gaped at her frowsily, and her belongings were scattered
around it in hopeless disorder. She'd have to do her homework in bed, she supposed. Daddy wouldn't want her not
to do it. She went to the bathroom to wash and when she
came out in her pajamas she heard the boys whispering
together in their room, and Catherine and Angela giggling
in theirs. Only Patsy was alone. Her heart was full of
rebellious feelings.

It hadn't been her fault. No one had told her to look
after the little ones. They had always been all right before,
playing in the garden. How was she to know that Timmy
would get it into his head to light a bonfire? You could
never guess what that boy would dream up next. Miss
Thorpe had realized that Joan was busy because she had
been *doing* something. No one ever thought *talking* was
anything. Yet finding out what had happened to Peter had
been important too, Patsy felt. She snorted with anger,
though deep down she felt miserable. Daddy's opinion
mattered a great deal to her, and Daddy had said she

dodged responsibility. Patsy knew that there was truth in it—maybe not this time, but at other times. There was her unmade bed, for instance—and if she had put her knitting away more carefully, and had not been late, this morning's trouble would not have happened. Patsy heaved a deep sigh. Downstairs the grandfather clock ticked monotonously.

A great longing for Mother overwhelmed Patsy. Mother knew all about her; she knew Patsy's faults, but they didn't matter. Mother knew what Patsy really *wanted* to be like, and, with Mother, Patsy seemed to be that ideal little girl. But she must not go to Mother. It was forbidden.

Patsy looked around her. No one saw her. There was a steady murmur of voices downstairs. She tiptoed to Mother's bedroom door and listened. Light shone through the keyhole. Gently she turned the knob and peeked in. There was Mother, propped against her pillow, peacefully reading a book. She looked soft and sweet in her pink bed jacket. The room was bathed in the rosy light of the bedside lamp. Mother looked up, and her face warmed when she saw Patsy. She put a finger to her lips and pointed at the cradle. Patsy nodded and tiptoed into the room. She knelt by Mother's bed. She put her head on the coverlet, so that its candlewick tufts pressed into her cheek. Mother stroked her hair. Patsy felt tears stinging her eyelids.

"I couldn't *bear* it," she choked. "I *had* to see you!"

She knew she must not say any more, must not worry Mother with her troubles. Mother kept stroking her hair with a rhythmic motion, and the tight knot in Patsy's heart slowly relaxed. She began to breathe more quietly. Mother kept stroking for a long time; then she whispered,

"I'm being naughty, having you here. We'll keep this visit a secret, shall we?"

Patsy looked up, a delighted smile on her face. Fancy *Mother's* feeling guilty! And what fun, to be wicked together with Mother!

It was hard to leave, it felt so safe in Mother's room, but she knew she had to, so she kissed Mother quietly and sneaked out again, closing the door softly.

When she came to her room she found it all tidy; her bed had been made and there was a little note pinned to her blanket.

"Miss Thorpe was unfair," it said. "Catherine and I made your bed. Love, Angela."

FOUR

"Homework"

THE next day was much better because Mother wanted to see Timmy the moment she woke up, and whatever she said to him turned him into a regular little knight; he came prancing downstairs as if on a steed and even asked Miss Thorpe if he could shine her shoes for her!

Joan had got up earlier and had breakfast ready. Daddy seemed more genial too.

He talked seriously to the children, saying that he expected them to realize that they all had to help. Mother was no longer young and needed extra care. There were two babies instead of one, which added to the strain and the expense. They could not afford a maid, and Miss

Thorpe wasn't there to do housework. So they'd just have
to learn to manage by themselves. It was a change for
them, of course. Mother had spoiled them all, looking
after them so well, and that's why he felt he might have
been too severe with them last night. But that would do
no harm if it made them realize that he would stand no
nonsense. He wanted order and peace in the house, and if
there wasn't, no matter whose fault it was, he'd punish
the lot.

Miss Thorpe stood in the background and kept nod-
ding her head. The only time she didn't nod was when
Daddy said he might have been too severe.

But Mother must have put in a good word for them, for
from then on, they were allowed to see her in turns.
Angela was asked to bring up her breakfast tray, Catherine helped serve lunch when the others were at school,
and Peter was to carry up her supper. Timmy had two
visits: first thing in the morning and again at three in the
afternoon, to tell his good news. Patsy's time was in the
evening after her homework was done. Joan offered to be
Miss Thorpe's assistant, as Miss Thorpe said she badly
needed one. So Joan had free access to Mother's room.
She was also to look after the supper in the future, which
was a pleasure, for she loved trying her hand at cakes and
pies.

All the same, there was something wrong with Joan. It
must have been because of the way Miss Thorpe but-
tered her up.

"Joan is such a help; she is so dependable . . . I don't
know what I'd do without her . . ."—that sort of thing. It
would have been all right if Joan had boasted about it;
that would have been *normal*. But she did nothing of the
kind. She became all angelic and sweet, with a sort of

holy smile. That's what the other children couldn't stand.

The trouble with Miss Thorpe was that she had all sorts of rules in her head which she expected the children to know. Perhaps they were English rules. They were new to the Mitchells anyway. Rules about eating and talking, washing and getting up and sitting down and saying "Please" and "Excuse me." These rules were all right in their way, but the younger Mitchell children felt that Miss Thorpe made too much fuss about them. They felt persecuted.

So they made themselves a refuge. There was only one place safe from Miss Thorpe's eyes, and that was the attic. Miss Thorpe hadn't discovered it because you had to get there by way of a deep closet on the second floor, where suitcases and screens were stored. There was a ladder in it, leading to a trap door; when you pushed that open you could climb into the attic. The children hadn't been there for ages. It was a scary place, full of cobwebs and dust, but even spiders were better than Miss Thorpe. And it was rather a thrilling place too, full of dark corners and boxes and trunks and broken furniture. The children were quite happy exploring it, after they had got used to the dim atmosphere. Peter found an old sword—perhaps it had belonged to Daddy, or to Uncle Jim. Uncle Jim had been killed in the last war. There was also the cage for poor Mr. Jenkins their parrot, who hadn't been able to survive the Canadian winter.

It was Angela who proposed, "Let's build a hut here, where no one can find us!"

The others thought that was a splendid idea. They chose the corner with one of the windows, the one that looked out over the snowy fields at the back of the house.

They piled up boxes to make a wall. They found some old curtains which made another wall. Patsy fetched a broom and swept their piece of floor clean. She also destroyed some cobwebs, but one spider was so big that Patsy got frightened and Peter had to finish the job.

They found a spare bed, which did very well for a sofa, with a gay printed spread on it. They found the spread in a trunk, as well as some old blankets. They found a piece of carpet too, and a three-legged chair, which could be propped up with an empty orange crate. Two trunks made a good bench and a table.

When they had finished they were all very dirty. They went to supper with cobwebs in their hair, and were promptly sent back by Miss Thorpe to brush them out.

"She notices *everything*," they grumbled.

Joan wanted to know where they'd been, but they didn't tell. It must be kept a secret. If Miss Thorpe found out they'd never be free of her. She seemed to think it her duty to know everything they were doing, and ever since the bonfire she kept asking them where they were going and why; therefore they had agreed beforehand to call their hiding place "Homework." Then it wouldn't be lying to say they had been at their homework, if she asked.

There was another reason why they badly needed a hideout. None of their possessions was safe any more. Miss Thorpe had simply *no* sense of values. She threw away all Timmy's paper soldiers, which he had been cutting out of magazines for months—and they couldn't leave a comic book lying about anywhere. Miss Thorpe disapproved of comics. And she even actually threw Traincrack into the *garbage!* Traincrack was a doll Angela had owned since she was three, and it had become a kind of idol. With its wigless head and gnomelike body, it resembled an

Indian fakir. Angela was still devoted to it and sought its comfort in moments of depression. If one of its legs had not stuck out from under the lid of the garbage can, the poor doll might have been lost forever. As it was, Angela only discovered it in the nick of time. But now they could take all their treasures up to the attic.

Catherine had to be left out because Miss Thorpe concentrated too much on her, and they were afraid she was too young to keep a secret.

Poor Catherine! She was already very much under Miss Thorpe's thumb. She had to wash her teeth three times a day, and her hands far oftener. Miss Thorpe did her hair in a different way to keep it out of her eyes. When she brushed it, she pulled so hard that poor Catherine's head was jerked back and forth. If Catherine dirtied her frock or ate vegetables with her fingers, Miss Thorpe made her stand in the corner. Catherine didn't seem to protest very much. Perhaps she thought it was useless, or perhaps she enjoyed all the attention. But once Patsy heard her murmuring sadly to herself, "I'm going to be a baby. I'm going to cry and drink milk, and everyone will stand in a row to look at me and call me *twins*." It was hard to be only three.

The others soon learned to dodge Miss Thorpe's excessive demands. If she had had her way, the Mitchells would have spent most of their time at the washbasin.

"England must be a dreary place," said Peter one afternoon, when they were together in Homework. "I guess everybody is always clean there."

"The Bastable children weren't clean, and *they* were English," Angela pointed out.

"Well then, Miss Thorpe never met the Bastable children, that's clear," said Peter. "Let's play a game."

He and Timmy had raided the kitchen while Miss

Thorpe was bringing Mother her tea. They had brought up half a pie, a bottle of milk, and a box of crackers. Miss Thorpe didn't approve of their eating between meals. It was no use telling her that Mother always let them have something when they came home from school.

"It just means extra cleaning up," said Miss Thorpe, "and it's a bad habit. Your stomach needs a rest."

"But my stomach *isn't* resting," Timmy had complained. "It's biting me!"

So now they had their bad habit in the attic. They felt lovely and cozy. Eating forbidden food is always fun, and having to whisper (for fear of giving their secret away) gave the party a delightful air of conspiracy.

"Let's do the guessing game," said Patsy. "You may go out first, Peter, and plug up your ears, or it's not fair."

The others put their heads together and agreed on a person.

"Ready!" they cried.

Peter came back. He had buckled on the sword. "What kind of flower is it like?" he asked.

"A thistle," said Patsy.

"And what kind of animal?"

"A crab!" cried Timmy.

"Hush," said Patsy, "don't talk so loud or they'll hear you downstairs." Timmy took fright and clapped his hand over his mouth.

"What kind of fruit?"

"A prune," said Angela.

"What kind of food?"

"Soup," said Patsy.

"Oh, *Miss Thorpe*—that was too easy." Peter laughed. The others applauded softly.

"May I go out now?" asked Timmy, darting off.

The others huddled together again.

"Ready!" they called.

Timmy's face was flushed, and his eyes sparkled with ambition. He was always trying to outdo Peter, and, of course, never succeeded. "What kind of flower is it like?" he asked.

"A dandelion." Angela chuckled.

"And what kind of animal?"

"A little brown bear," said Peter.

"Hmm." Timmy frowned. He didn't know anybody like a little brown bear. "What kind of food?" he asked.

"A sausage," said Angela.

"No, a jellied doughnut," corrected Patsy.

"That's too sweet," said Angela.

"Well, a sausage is too heavy," argued Patsy.

"Listen," warned Peter, "you're not to discuss it like that or he'll find out."

But Timmy wasn't anywhere near finding out. He looked very puzzled. "What kind of fruit?" he asked.

"Oh . . . an apple." They were all agreed on that.

"And what kind of—a—a—house?"

"An igloo," said Patsy.

"We-ell—what—what kind of insect?" faltered Timmy, completely at sea.

"A bumblebee."

"It's not—one of the twins?" asked Timmy.

They all laughed. "Do you give it up?"

But Timmy wouldn't give it up for a long time, though they finally had to tell him it was himself.

"That's not fair," he cried, "I don't know myself!" which made them all laugh again.

It was getting too dark to stay in the attic; besides, their insides warned them that it would soon be suppertime, and Joan or Miss Thorpe might be looking for them. So they crept downstairs, very softly, and listened carefully at the closet door before they opened it. They had already decided what they would say if someone saw them coming out: they'd say they were playing hide-and-seek—they were, weren't they, from Miss Thorpe? But no one saw them. Mother must have heard them, though, for she called, "Children!"

Patsy opened the door of her bedroom and peeked in. Mother was *alone!* Miss Thorpe and Joan must both have gone downstairs. Mother had a guilty look on her face as she beckoned Patsy to come in. Peter stuck his head in after her, and Mother beckoned to him too, but put her finger to her lips. So, like conspirators, all four children entered the room, Timmy as quietly as he could, though his efforts made him blow like a porpoise.

Mother looked at them with delight. "I just *had* to find out what you were doing," she whispered. "You were in the attic, weren't you?"

The children glanced at one another. How did Mother know?

"I heard you," she said. "It's right over my head here. Miss Thorpe heard something too, but I told her we had lots of mice." She winked at them. That made them want to tell her everything.

"We built a hut," they whispered. "It's a secret—don't tell."

"Oh no, I won't," promised Mother. "But it's a bit cold up there, isn't it?"

Yes, they had to admit it: it *was* cold there. Now that Mother mentioned it, they realized they were all shivering. Angela even had blue lips.

"Look, if you *promise* to be careful," whispered Mother,

"and to remember to pull the plug out when you leave, and not to put it near paper—or anything flammable— you may have my electric heater. Peter, it's in that clothes closet there—get it out, will you, honey? Yes—no, that's the wrong side—behind the shoe rack, to the left there. Mind my best dress! Yes, that's it." For Peter had found the little round electric heater, with a cage in front of its face and the cord wound like a tail round its leg.

"Oh, *Mommy!*" he cried. "The *very* thing!"

"But *do* be careful, dear," said Mother a little anxiously.

"I'm eleven, you know," Peter assured her. "I accept the responsibility. Thanks a lot." Then he bent over and kissed her. "That was so *mother* of you," he said warmly.

The others had been peeking into the cradle where the twins were lying like two furled rosebuds. One little rosebud unfurled slightly, flailed out a tiny fist, and hit the other in the eye. The other opened his mouth and let out a wail.

"Mommy, they're *fighting!*" cried Timmy, delighted. "They really *are* boys!" He had doubted it up till now, what with those dresses and ribbons.

"Shall I bring you the baby?" asked Patsy, anxious to help, but Mother shook her head.

"No, dear, you'd better go now. Miss Thorpe will be coming up and she must not find you here." As the children slid quietly out of the room, they wondered if Mother was afraid of Miss Thorpe too!

Peter hid the electric heater in his room, under his bedclothes, till he had a chance to take it to the attic. He realized that he'd have to get an extension cord to work it, as the attic bulb was outside their hut. After supper he rummaged in the kitchen drawers and found one.

It was dull downstairs in the evening. Daddy wasn't jolly and funny, the way he usually was. He buried himself in his newspaper, while Miss Thorpe sat near the lamp, doing embroidery. But Daddy could not read in comfort because Miss Thorpe kept making conversation all the time.

Miss Thorpe: "Did you find it cold out today?"
Daddy (with one eye on the paper): "No, a bit sharp, perhaps, but not colder than usual."
Miss Thorpe: "Well, it seemed to me it was colder. I could see my breath when I took the milk in."
Daddy: "It's always like that in the morning. I don't think it was more than ten degrees below freezing."
Miss Thorpe: "That's cold enough."
Daddy: "It's still March; what can you expect?"
Miss Thorpe: "I expect spring."
Daddy: "I gather you haven't lived here long."
Miss Thorpe: "Oh no, I'm from England, where we have a *much* milder climate."
Daddy: "Yes, fog all the time."

The children crept out of the room. They had done their homework and were ready for Homework now. They were longing to try the heater. Peter had the cord and plug. They sneaked upstairs. Joan was with Mother; they could hear her reading aloud. For a moment they all envied her, but then they remembered the heater. They peeked into Angela's room and saw that Catherine was fast asleep in her crib.

The heater was wonderful. The only trouble was that you couldn't use the electric light at the same time, so Peter had brought his flashlight. The attic wasn't the sort

of place you'd want to be alone in after dark, but when
there were four of you it was all right. Still, there was a
scary moment, before the heater shed its rosy glow, when
the flashlight went out. The moon shone like a ghost
through the cobwebby window, making strange, eerie
shadows—then the heater lit up like a rising sun and
they crouched around its cheerful warmth.

"It's just the place for a story," whispered Angela.

"A rigmarole," said Timmy.

"All right," agreed Peter. "You start, Patsy."

Patsy leaned back on a dusty old cushion and began.

"Long, long ago there were a king and a queen who
lived happily in an old castle. The king went out hunting
every day and the queen sewed beautiful garments and
ate sugar plums out of a crystal dish. Then one day the
postman brought them a letter. It was from an old aunt, a
kind of witch, who wanted to visit them.

" 'Don't let her come,' said the queen. 'She'll make
trouble for us.'

" 'She is my aunt,' said the king. 'It is my duty.'

" 'Well, don't say I didn't warn you,' said the queen.

"It turned out just as she had feared. The moment the
old witch came into the castle, their peace was over. She
brought with her twelve large, venomous toads which
gave off such a bad smell that the whole place became
uninhabitable. The king and queen had to retire to their
highest turret room. You had to go up a winding staircase
to get there, and the toads were too fat and lazy to climb
it. So they had peace again, and besides, they had a wonderful view. They were so much nearer heaven that they
could see the angels fly in and out of the Pearly Gates,
and that made them very happy.

" 'We were never so cozy before,' said the queen, who

had turned up her petticoats to get more warmth from the stove.

" 'Yes,' said the king, loosening his ermine collar and hanging his heavy crown on a nail. 'Our life is much nicer now. I see so much more of *you,* dear—and do you remember all those dreary visits we had to make and all those dull people we had to entertain? Now I only write an occasional letter to the Prime Minister and he does the rest of the work. I think we'll stay here.'

"But, alas, the old aunt discovered where they were, and up she came, panting and puffing. She made a dreadful fuss.

" 'I call it rotten bad manners!' she shrieked. '*I'm* the guest, and instead of entertaining me, you leave me alone in that horrid big palace with your rude servants. Sneaky, that's what I call it, and selfish too!'

"Of course this made the king and queen blush, for they had been told from the time they sucked their thumbs that they must *never* be selfish. The king cleared his throat.

" 'It's the toads,' he said. 'I never could abide toads. Get rid of them and I'll treat you as an honored guest.'

"But here the old aunt broke down. 'They are all I have,' she sobbed. 'Just twelve teenie weenie little froggies, and you begrudge them to me.'

"This made the king and queen feel worse than ever. They promised the old aunt that she could do what she liked and they followed her downstairs with bowed backs . . . Now it's your turn, Peter."

"Oh dear," said Peter, who had been waiting to hear what would happen next. "Wee-ell," he began, frowning and staring into the red eye of the heater, "the real trouble, of course, was that the king had followed the queen's advice. That was a fool thing for a king to do, to be skulking in an attic when he had a whole big country to rule. A moment's thought made him realize this, so he asked a couple of scientists to come to the palace and he had a practical sort of talk with them while the queen was walking in the garden with the aunt. They said they could easily perform an operation on the toads to take away their poison glands, which made the bad smell.

" 'It won't hurt them at all,' they said. 'We'd put them to sleep.'

"But the aunt wouldn't hear of it, so, thank goodness, she went off in a huff, taking the toads with her.

"Meanwhile, the king had learned something in the attic. He realized that he had never been a proper king. All he'd done was hunt and give parties. He repented of his foolishness and consulted again with the scientists. They built him an elegant little two-engine monoplane, equipped with telescopes and radar. Now he could fly over his kingdom and discover the most amazing secrets. He even found some traitors who wanted to dethrone him, but he was merciful. He didn't shoot them; he just sent them to a school to teach them how to rule a country, and they had to learn so much geography and history they didn't want to be king any more. . . . Now you, Timmy."

"We-ell," began Timmy, blinking and heaving a deep breath, "The king was good. He saw some poor people and he said to his page, 'Go, bring me a hundred bags of gold out of the cellar, and get my velvet clothes out of the cupboard, and some of my second-best crowns. Oh, and get some large pies from the cook and some roast turkey.' And he gave them all to the poor and . . . the queen . . . took off her jewels . . . and gave . . . them . . .

to the poor . . . too." Timmy stopped; his eyelids were drooping.

Angela gave him a poke. "Go on," she said.

"Well," said Timmy sleepily, "the king was so good that it was mean of someone to put a bomb in the palace, but it did happen, and it went off with a loud bang, and there was a hole, but no one was killed. But it might happen again, so the king told his guards to look out for suspicious caricatures. But . . . they . . . couldn't find any. . . . It's your turn now, Angela." Timmy yawned. It was past his bedtime.

"It was a dragon," said Angela briskly. "He lived in the next-door country and he wanted to fight the king. The king was very brave, and so were his soldiers, but the dragon kept on winning. Then the king thought of the toads. He was glad their poison glands hadn't been removed. He gave them armor and weapons and sent them into the dragon's country and they made such a bad smell that the dragon crawled into his hole in the ground and didn't come out for ten years. The king was so proud of the toads that he made them into knights and had a special palace built for them, and they got to be much appreciated for they had used up all their smell on the dragon, and because they had been misunderstood they took care of all the unpopular animals in the kingdom, and they built an animal hospital and made the old aunt the head of it, and no animal was ever unhappy in the kingdom again."

"And that's all Angela cares about," said Patsy, laughing. There was a gentle snore from Timmy, who was curled up on the sofa, fast asleep.

"Oh dear, we'll have to wake him. How'll we get him down?" Patsy said anxiously. She prodded Timmy, but that had no effect. Timmy was the hardest person to rouse, once he was asleep. But by applying various methods of torture they finally got him awake and Patsy and Peter managed to haul him downstairs between them. Angela came last—she had unplugged the heater. They had just put Timmy to bed when they saw Joan coming out of Mother's room.

"Hullo, where were you all?" she asked, surprised. "I was looking for you. Mommy wanted Patsy, but when I said you weren't downstairs or in your room, she said, 'Never mind,' so it wasn't important. But where *were* you?"

"At our Homework," chorused the others virtuously.

FIVE

The Fight

PETER could not understand why Paul Lepine had suddenly turned a gang against him. Paul was new; he had attended Peter's school only since Christmas. From the beginning he had seemed to dislike the English-speaking boys, and especially Peter, because he was from the States. This seemed silly to Peter. What did it matter where you came from or what language you spoke? It was the sort of person you were that mattered. Peter had made great friends among the French boys. He liked learning French. Someday he wanted to travel and see the world. He wanted to find out about the different customs and manners of foreign countries. Already he had enjoyed the difference between Canada and the United States. He especially liked the Canadian winters, with their dramatic cold spells and thick, blinding blizzards. Canada was a man's country, where you mustn't be afraid of getting a frozen toe.

Peter had gaped at first to see the plows clearing the street after a snowstorm. Like big white fountains, the superfluous snow had been sprayed into the Mitchells' garden, making wonderful deep hills through which you could dig tunnels. Then there had been snowball battles. Peter at first could not understand why the Canadian boys always won, until he found out that they made their ammunition in advance. They had caches of snowballs everywhere, hidden in the banks on either side of the road. So while he wasted time making the balls, they kept pelting. After that, Peter had his own caches. That was all fun. But this business with Paul was serious. He really seemed to hate Peter.

On the Friday morning after the twins' birth Peter was sitting on his bench at the front of the class, and Paul, also in front, was sitting a few desks away. Peter felt that Paul often glared in his direction. It gave him an uncomfortable feeling.

Monsieur Brabant, the teacher, was a wiry little Frenchman with deep-set brown eyes and hair stiffly erect in a brush cut. He was entertaining the class with lively tales about the early days in Canada's history; about the gallant soldier Maisonneuve who founded the settlement called

Ville Marie, which later became Montreal. He told of the religious fervor of the first settlers; how the idea of building a city on Mount Royal had come in a dream to two people in Paris. When they met each other on the street, they recognized each other from their dreams and joined together to arrange the expedition. The first thing the settlers did was to plant a wooden cross on the top of Mount Royal, which was replaced as often as the Indians burned it. The next thing they wanted to do was to celebrate Mass. But they had no candles. So they thought of catching some of the numerous twinkling fireflies and imprisoning them in two glass containers. That way they had lights for their Mass. The teacher also told of the little dog Pilote, who could smell an Indian from afar, and went the rounds of the settlement every day to sniff out danger. Her warnings saved many lives. When she had puppies, they had to come too. They didn't want to, for it was a long walk and they had short legs, but Pilote made them. When one of the puppies ran away, she punished him severely afterward. So even the pioneer puppies led tough lives!

The teacher told it all so interestingly that Peter could see it happen.

Against the wall, behind the teacher's desk, stood a huge statue of St. Joseph, the patron saint of Canada. It was made of plaster, with glass eyes, and realistically painted. Everyone admired it very much. With this towering dignity behind him, the teacher looked particularly short and vivacious.

Monsieur Brabant often selected Peter to do jobs for him. That morning, he had noticed that the inkwells were drying out, so he asked Peter to fill them during recess.

"You'll find the bottle of ink in the supply cupboard," he said.

Peter was pleased. Lately recess had not been much fun, with Paul and his gang lying in wait for him.

Why did Paul hate him so? He'd never done anything to justify such a feeling. Peter puzzled about it as he fetched the big bottle of ink from the cupboard in the hall. When he returned he could hear the noise of boys shouting in the playground. The window was open a bit, to let in fresh air.

The classroom seemed strangely still, like the shell from which an animal has gone. But possessions lay scattered about. Some boys had left sweaters on their benches; books and copybooks lay open on the desks. Peter went from one desk to another, filling inkwells. He had just arrived at Paul's desk when a noise startled him and he spilled ink over Paul's books.

"Look what you're doing, stupid Yankee!" cried a furious voice.

Peter looked up and saw Paul glaring at him, his cheeks an angry red.

"It was your own fault for scaring me," said Peter calmly, looking for a piece of blotting paper.

Paul jumped at him from behind. Luckily Peter had just put down the ink bottle, otherwise more damage might have been done. He jerked himself out of Paul's grasp and struck him on the jaw. Paul gave him an answering punch on the nose. Soon they were at it fast and furious. It was what Peter had wanted, a fair fight. Paul's bodyguard was nowhere to be seen. But Peter was surprised at Paul's ferocity. He'd thought of Paul as a coward, but Paul wasn't fighting like a coward.

There wasn't enough elbow room between the benches,

so they instinctively moved to the front of the class. Peter's nose was bleeding, but he barely noticed it, he was so busy matching Paul's blows. He finally managed to push Paul down, and they rolled over and over on the floor, Peter getting madder all the time, especially when he felt Paul's teeth in his wrist. One moment one boy was on top, then the other. They were soon covered with powdered chalk as they struggled in front of the blackboards. Finally Peter tore loose and jumped up. Paul leaped up after him and gave Peter a hard push. Peter reeled, clawing for support. He fell against the statue, which tottered on its stand. There was a breathless moment as the huge, unwieldy figure swayed uncertainly—then it crashed down with a thundering noise on the teacher's desk and collapsed in a rubble of plaster, one glass eye rolling the length of the room.

Peter sat amidst the debris in a daze. He realized that the statue had missed him by inches and that he might have been killed if it had hit him. It had certainly made a dent in the desk. He felt himself to see whether he was still all there. He was, though dusted with plaster. His nose was still bleeding, and he held his handkerchief against it. Then he looked around for Paul, but Paul had vanished. He had left Peter to face the music alone, and what a tune it was! An atom bomb could not have created more of a sensation when the class returned after recess and found out what had happened.

Amid the excitement the teacher came in, and how was Peter to explain to this outraged man that he had managed to knock over a six-foot statue, as well as acquire a bleeding nose, all in the process of filling inkwells? The teacher naturally wanted to know who else was involved. Peter would not tell. True to his code, he would admit only that the statue had "got in the way" when he was filling the inkwells.

"Are you trying to tell me," asked Monsieur Brabant sarcastically, "that you had a fight with Saint Joseph?"

A titter ran through the class. The boys were taut with suspense. It was like living a mystery story, with a corpse and a suspect. Peter slid a glance at Paul, expecting him to stand and own up. But Paul cowered in his seat. He had tidied himself sufficiently so his appearance did not betray him. As no amount of investigating brought Monsieur Brabant closer to the truth, he finally told Peter to make himself presentable and report to Monsieur Leger, the headmaster, and to bring a broom with him when he returned.

Peter had to spend some time in the washroom, for his nosebleed had done a lot of damage to his shirt and suit. But he managed to get the worst of the spots off, and he beat the dust out of his coat and combed his hair. He still looked rather battered when he went to the headmaster.

Monsieur Leger took a grave view of the matter.

"The statue was given to us by a prominent member of the school board," he said, adjusting his spectacles. "We dare not offend him. Personally, I think the church is the place for statues, not school. This accident proves it. You might have been badly hurt. Though it would have been your own fault," he added, glaring at Peter through his thick lenses. "However, as I said, we dare not offend this gentleman, so the statue will have to be replaced." He twirled his grizzled mustache and frowned at Peter.

Peter gulped. "Is it very expensive?"

Monsieur Leger raised his bushy eyebrows and spread out his hands. "But of course," he said. "It may cost you a hundred dollars, and your father is not rich. He has many children. Do you want to let him in for such an expense?"

"Does the statue have to be exactly the same?" asked Peter, licking his dry lips.

"It would be better, if possible. I don't know if they still make them like that. This statue was at least ten years old."

Peter looked worried. Monsieur Leger pointed a blunt forefinger at him. "You know very well that you did not do this alone," he said accusingly. "I do not believe you even started it. This is the second year you have been at this school, and I have been well satisfied with you. You're a good student and you have always behaved courteously. If you tell me who the other boys were, you won't have to bear the penalty alone. Your father will have less to pay. It will make a great difference, believe me." Monsieur Leger's voice had a coaxing sound. He wanted very much to know the whole truth about this affair.

Peter felt tempted. Surely it wasn't fair that he should have to pay for the whole statue. Why hadn't Paul owned up? It couldn't be worse for Paul than it was for Peter. All the same, you didn't tell on a classmate. It just wasn't done.

The headmaster saw Peter's resolute expression. He sighed. "Very well then," he said in a resigned tone. "You may go. But I must warn you that the statue will have to be replaced before the next meeting of the school board, which will take place in this building."

"When is that?" asked Peter.

"In three weeks' time."

When Peter returned to his classroom, armed with a broom, the teacher made him sweep up all the broken pieces of the statue and carry them down to the dustbin in the basement. Then he gave him an essay to write on "Respect for Public Property." All the time Paul sat comfortably on his bench, looking as if he'd been picking daisies.

Peter waited for Patsy outside the convent school. He wanted to tell her what had happened. He could trust Patsy. Joan was no good; she told everything to Mother, and Mother must not hear of this. It would worry her dreadfully. Daddy would have to be told, of course, unless he and Patsy found another way out.

The girls were streaming out of school. Many wore the gay traditional Red River suits of Quebec: navy-blue coats with pointed hoods and woolen caps; leggings, mittens, and scarfs in either bright red or bright blue. They made vivid splashes of color against the snow.

There was Joan, walking with a friend.

"Hullo, what are you doing here?" she asked Peter.

"Oh, I just wanted to see what your school looks like," said Peter evasively.

"You know," the friend said to Joan as they walked on, "that brother of yours is going to be handsome."

"Peter?" asked Joan. "Goodness, I don't call that handsome—those big sticky-out ears, and that straight hair. And didn't you see his black eye? He must have been fighting again."

"You wait and see," said her companion.

Peter congratulated himself at having put the girls off. Then he noticed Angela, in the midst of a twittering group of friends. She didn't see him; so much the better. He noticed proudly that she looked prettier than most of the other girls; her hair was like a splash of sunlight. Ah, at last! There was Patsy, as harum-scarum as usual! That's what he loved about Patsy; she wasn't always dolling up. He gave the special whistle they had used since they were small children and Patsy looked up.

"Hi ya, Peter!" She ran to him with a glad smile. "Nice of you to wait for me!"

"I'm in trouble," said Peter. "I want to discuss it with you. But keep your mouth shut at home, will you?"

"Of course," agreed Patsy, who always kept Peter's secrets. She glanced anxiously at his black eye. "Paul again?"

Peter nodded. "In a way. Let's walk home; it saves car-fare, and I'm in desperate need of money at present."

"All right. Then you can have mine too."

"Thanks," said Peter.

They swung easily into their accustomed stride. Peter launched into a description of what had happened, and Patsy responded with gratifying concern and indignation.

"You might have been killed!" she exclaimed. "What a horrid boy that Paul is!"

"He certainly ducked his share of the blame," said Peter ruefully. "Boy, did he get out of that neatly!"

"He should have had all the blame; it was his fault entirely," declared Patsy.

But Peter pointed out that he had been fighting too. "I gave him a few good socks," he remembered with satisfaction. "But Paul bit me." And he showed Patsy the mark of Paul's teeth on his wrist.

"What can he have against you?" Patsy wondered. "He sounds like a wild beast."

"He fought like a wild beast," said Peter grimly. "But what am I to do now? I haven't got a hundred dollars—

and I don't want to ask Daddy for it if I can help it. Can you think of a way of earning money?"

"I have five dollars—" Patsy began. They had been amassed by dimes and quarters, as she had hoped to get a pair of skis next winter. "Perhaps the others can help."

"And where would that get us?" grumbled Peter. "It's a drop in the bucket."

"Perhaps we could get a second-hand statue—or—I know! Let's ask Pierre!"

"Pierre?" Peter looked puzzled.

"Pierre Jolicoeur—*you* know, from Sainte-Félice. He works in Monsieur Latour's shop, don't you remember? He *makes* statues."

"Oh!" Peter felt ashamed to have forgotten their old friend. "Of course! That's a splendid idea!"

Meanwhile, at home, Timmy had come stomping up the stairs.

"Good news, Mommy, good news!"

"Him again," grumbled Miss Thorpe. Mother raised herself up a little. She was very thin, and her eyes looked tired. The babies had been keeping her awake at night.

"Good news, Mommy!" Timmy burst into the room like a bomb. Energy streamed from him and seemed to quicken the air about him. "Her name isn't Philosophy!" he shouted.

Miss Thorpe put her fingers in her ears. "Spare us, child," she said. "We're not deaf."

"She's called *Felicity*," Timmy continued a little more softly.

"Well, that *is* a mercy," observed Miss Thorpe.

"Yes, and she gave me this," said Timmy. He extracted a small object from his pocket. It was wrapped in silver paper. Timmy undid it reverently and showed Mother a big yellowish-white bone button with four holes in it.

"My goodness, what did she give you that for?" asked Mother, surprised.

Timmy felt a lack of appreciation and hastily wrapped the button up again. He stowed it away tenderly in his pocket. "Because she had nothing else, of course," he said. His face glowed with gratitude. "Mommy, I want to give her something too, but I need money."

Mother reached for the black bag that hung on the knob of her bed. She gave him a quarter and told him to run along now, for the babies had to be fed.

Timmy knew that twenty-five cents wasn't enough for his purpose. He wasn't going to give Felicity just an ordinary present. No, it had to be very special. Timmy had thought about it for several days now, and he had decided that he was going to give her a golden bicycle. That was the only present that seemed to suit the glamour of her personality. What do people do when they need money? There was a lucky fellow called Aladdin who had only to rub a lamp. But it didn't work on the lamps in Timmy's house. Timmy had tried them.

Timmy trudged up to Homework. There was nobody there yet. He brooded for a while without finding a solution. Meanwhile he rolled the quarter along the floor. He rolled it back and forth until it fell into a crack. Then he cried because he could not get it out.

When Angela came up she said she knew of a way to get it. She used the wire of a clothes hanger and pried about in the crack until she got the quarter up. Timmy was so glad that he confided his plans to her. But Angela was suspicious of this female character whom Timmy was introducing into their lives.

"What's this Felicity like? Has she curls?" she asked.

"No." Timmy shook his head.

"Well, has she blond hair then?"

"No." Timmy couldn't say that she had.

"Has she blue eyes?" Angela cross-examined further.

"No."

"Then what's so good about her?" asked Angela.

Timmy reflected for a while. "I don't think blue eyes and blond curls would *suit* her," he said at last.

Daddy came home early that Friday night. He had a plan for the next day: they were going to visit the Jolicoeurs.

Of course Daddy did not know that this was providential as far as Peter and Patsy were concerned. His idea was to relieve the congestion at home over the weekend. Miss Thorpe had told him that Mother needed far more rest than she was getting. The twins were suffering from colic and crying a lot. Somehow Miss Thorpe connected this with children slamming doors and shouting.

"I think mothers of large families should have their babies in the hospital," she told Daddy severely.

But Daddy knew that Mother hated hospitals, and he thought that the children upset Miss Thorpe far more than they did their mother, who was used to them. All the same, he felt it might be good strategy to take them up north for Saturday. Mother applauded it too. She said that a day with only the twins and Miss Thorpe would be a lovely change.

So Daddy went to inspect Sweet Chariot, the Mitchells' old car, to see if it would weather the journey. It was called Sweet Chariot because it had always carried them home in spite of all appearances. It was so old that there were holes in the floor and you had to be careful where you put your feet when you got in. One of the headlights squinted because of a minor collision, and the horn had a cold. But Daddy said the engine was all right.

He had phoned the Jolicoeurs, who had invited them all to a sugaring-off party—probably the last one of this season, they said.

The children had never been to one, and were wildly excited. Peter tried to coax Miss Thorpe to dance around the kitchen with him. She protested loudly, but she didn't look as annoyed as usual, Patsy observed.

"We'll take sandwiches," commanded Daddy. "You make them, Joan, and put in a couple of bottles of milk, and hard-boiled eggs—and paper napkins." Daddy looked very proud of himself after these instructions, and Joan laughed. As if she did not know how to pack a picnic far better than Daddy!

As she was slicing tomatoes for sandwiches after supper (they'd have to leave early the next morning if they were to have any time with the Jolicoeurs) she heard Patsy and Peter whispering to each other. They made a sign and disappeared. Timmy and Angela followed. Only Catherine was left in the kitchen. She was still eating her dessert.

Joan frowned. They had a secret, those others. She was sure they had. They would allude mysteriously to their homework—as if that were anything special—and during supper they'd been giggling about jokes Joan didn't understand. She hoped they weren't up to something. She felt she ought to tell Mother. But when she went upstairs to Mother's room she found her and Miss Thorpe earnestly discussing the twins' christening clothes. Miss Thorpe was holding up the beautiful long robe in which all the other Mitchell babies had been baptized. It had a long skirt of soft Limerick lace, and little puffed sleeves. But, as Mother pointed out sadly, only one of the twins could wear it.

"We'll have to draw lots"—she sighed—"and the other will just have to wear an ordinary little short dress."

When Joan mentioned her suspicions about the children's secret, Mother didn't seem to listen. So Joan went back to the kitchen to finish her sandwiches. It won't be my fault if they're up to mischief, she thought.

She noticed that Catherine still hadn't finished her orange. "Why don't you eat it?" she asked irritably.

Catherine gave her a dark glance. "You've taken its skin off," she said, "and now it's crying." And she rocked it in her arms.

"You little silly," said Joan. She put a pan of water on the stove to boil eggs, and then she started to slice and butter another loaf. The tomato sandwiches were finished. Presently the egg sandwiches were finished too.

"It's your bedtime, Cathy," she warned. "Oh, where's the orange?"

Catherine looked at her smugly. "It isn't crying any more," she said. "It's in my tummy, and it's *happy!*"

Joan wrapped up the sandwiches. "Come to bed now," she said.

But to her chagrin, Catherine cried, "I want Angela to take me to bed; I like Angela."

Up till now Joan had always been Catherine's favorite sister, but during the last few days Joan had been so wrapped up in the newborn babies that she hadn't realized what was happening to the rest of the family. Now she began to awaken to the fact that she was losing her place there.

When she had tucked Catherine in bed she began to

explore the house. Where could the children be? Surely they wouldn't have gone outside—and anyway, their coats were hanging in the hall. They weren't in the cellar, either.

Daddy heard her puttering about. He called to her. "What's happened to my children?" he said. "I don't seem to have a family any more."

"No. I can't imagine, *where* they've all disappeared to," said Joan frowning.

"Did you tell Mother?"

"Yes, but she doesn't seem worried."

"Then we needn't worry either," said Daddy comfortably. "Come and sit here, and be my oldest daughter. I get lonesome too sometimes, you know!"

"You, Daddy? Oh no—*everybody* loves you," said Joan, sitting on the arm of his chair.

"Well, talk to me then," said Daddy.

When Joan went upstairs again she found that Peter, Timmy, Angela, and Patsy were all in their beds. They had reappeared as mysteriously as they had disappeared. Patsy was reading.

"Where were you?" asked Joan rather crossly, wriggling out of her dress.

"Wouldn't you like to know?" said Patsy.

"Now look, that won't do. You keep putting me off." Joan sat down on the edge of her bed and started to strip off her stockings. "Every time I ask you where you've been you give me a silly answer." Her lips trembled. Suddenly she flung herself on her pillow and began to cry. Her shoulders went up and down as she sobbed.

Patsy lowered her book and stared. Then she got out of bed and went to Joan. "What's the matter?" she asked. "Joanie, what's the matter?"

"What's the matter . . . what's the matter . . ." gulped

Joan. "As if you don't know! We've never had secrets from each other before. All of you act as if I didn't *belong* to you, just because I try to be useful—"

Patsy stood rooted to the ground. It was true. They *had* acted as if Joan didn't belong.

"But we thought you wanted to be a g-grownup—" she stammered.

Joan sat up and dried her eyes. She laughed a little. "Yes, I think I did," she admitted. "I did at first. I was pleased that Miss Thorpe liked me so much, but"—the tears began to flow again—"I don't want to lose all of you . . . I don't want to be left out of your secrets!" Joan wasn't a bit grown-up any more as she sat there, her nose red and her cheeks all wet. Patsy felt a sudden aching pity for her. It seemed that her splendid older sister wasn't as strong and sure as she pretended to be, that she could be very easily hurt. Patsy knew that she didn't want Joan to be hurt, ever.

"Shove over and I'll crawl into bed with you," she said, almost as if she were consoling a frightened Catherine. "Then we can talk, and I'll tell you all about it."

It was nice to be whispering together in the dark, and giggling over the name "Homework." Joan said it was a very good joke. She hadn't guessed a thing. "I did for a moment consider looking in the attic," she said, "but I thought it would be too scary and too cold there. You must have hated Miss Thorpe a lot to go up there. Brrr!"

"Don't you hate her?" asked Patsy.

"No, I think she is a decent soul, but she has been the nicest to me, of course," Joan admitted.

Patsy noticed that Joan wasn't being superior any more. She was a real sister again. "I'm glad," she said, hugging Joan, "I'm *so* glad you're back!"

SIX

Sugaring Off

ON SATURDAY the weather was lovely, mild and sunny. With some difficulty the Mitchells piled into Sweet Chariot, Joan and Catherine beside Daddy and the four middles in the back seat. There was the usual flurry of "Wait, Daddy, I forgot my galoshes!" "Go away, that was *my* place!" "Daddy, Daddy, Timmy *hit* me!" and they had trouble convincing Trusty that he had to stay behind. But they got off to an early start nevertheless, and everyone was in excellent humor. Joan was her old self again; the children noticed it, even though Patsy hadn't had time yet to tell the others what had happened the night before.

At first the road was very unattractive. Even in the sunshine it looked dreary, and there was a great deal of traffic, as always on the weekends. The landscape consisted mostly of flat farmland and even that was hidden by large advertising signs, temporary-looking frame buildings, and gas stations. Besides, the snow was melting, revealing mangy patches of bare earth here and there. But after they passed St. Jerome, the scenery began to improve. The road mounted and hills arched themselves on either side. Daddy began to sing, and the children joined in. They all felt as if they were playing hooky, Patsy thought. Perhaps it was because they had escaped from the sensible Miss Thorpe.

The higher they went, the deeper the snow looked, like a fat, downy quilt tucking in the countryside. Only the pine trees stuck out their dark spearheads like an army of soldiers. It was colder too.

"Do you all remember the Jolicoeurs?" Daddy asked, between songs.

"Yes, oh yes!" cried Joan, Patsy, and Peter. The other three didn't. Two years was too great a gap in their lives.

"There's Pierre," began Joan. "He was older than me."

"And Aline was a little younger than me," Patsy remembered. "Then there was George, a little younger than Peter, and Madeleine, a little younger than Angela. Noel was older than Timmy, but François was Timmy's age exactly—and the baby was younger than Catherine."

"We've one more now than they," crowed Peter. "Unless they've had another baby too."

"What's sugaring off, Daddy?" asked Timmy.

"You'll see, son," Daddy promised. "It's the way they make maple syrup."

They were driving through a wood with many maple

trees. Joan pointed to the shiny little tin cans hanging on their trunks. "They make a hole in the tree, put in a spigot, and the sap drips into the can. Isn't that right, Daddy?"

"Yes, and then they collect it in big containers, light a fire, and boil it. The water evaporates, and the sweet stuff that remains is syrup. This is perfect sugaring-off weather, warm and sunny in the daytime and cold at night. That makes the sap run."

The Jolicoeurs lived in a lovely old wooden farmhouse of the ancient French design, with a high, pointed roof. As the Mitchells went up the porch steps the Jolicoeur parents welcomed them cordially. They were having their midday meal, but would the Mitchells please join them?

The Mitchells explained that they had brought their own picnic (somewhat to the relief of the young Jolicoeurs, who for a moment had feared short rations). There was plenty of room at the Jolicoeurs' long table to fit in the Mitchells, if the children shoved up a little. Joan unpacked the sandwiches and poured out milk. Soon everyone was eating happily. The Mitchell children had been gazing at the Jolicoeur children, who looked very much the same as they remembered. They didn't even look much taller, because the Mitchells themselves had grown.

"But where is Pierre?" asked Patsy.

"Oh, Pierre is not back yet," said Mr. Jolicoeur, holding out his plate to his wife for more soup. "He doesn't get off so early on Saturday—much work in the shop," he added proudly.

"Pierre, 'e got a prize!" Mrs. Jolicoeur beamed. "Great prize for sculpture."

"Good work," applauded Daddy. "Who gave it to him?"

"Pierre studies at the École des Beaux Arts now, in the evening," explained Mr. Jolicoeur. "He earns by day and studies by night. Two years now, he studies at the École des Beaux Arts, and they give him the prize just now. It was in the papers." The Mitchells felt sorry that they had missed seeing it. "He has a scholarship," continued Mr. Jolicoeur. "He can study free, and he hopes to get another scholarship to travel to Rome."

It was obvious that the parents basked in the glory of their oldest son, and the other Jolicoeur children shared this feeling, for they sat listening with shining eyes and pleased smiles, exchanging little nudges and signs.

George slid from his bench and went to fetch a beautiful little carved wooden statue of an angel to show it to the Mitchells.

"Pierre did that," he said.

The other Jolicoeur children immediately hopped down and brought more samples of his work, until Maman told them to sit down and finish their dinner. But the Mitchells had seen enough to convince them that Pierre was a promising young artist and that his work had greatly improved in quality without losing the spontaneity of his earlier carvings.

"Monsieur Latour, 'e t'inks the world of Pierre, 'e wants 'im to be 'is partner—but Pierre not made up 'is mind. Pierre, 'e t'inks 'e like to travel, see the world." The mother smiled indulgently as she told this. It was clear that she considered it a pardonable weakness in her son which he was sure to overcome, and then he would settle down to a steady and respectable career in the shop. But the Mitchell children could see Pierre's point.

How much more entrancing to travel and have adventures, and maybe become famous, like Michelangelo, than to spend your life selling statues!

After dinner the children went outside. There was sugarbush all around the house. The sun was so hot that the snow was melting. The sound of dripping icicles mingled with the *plunk!-plunk!-ting!-ting!* of sap dripping into the tin pails.

Ste.-Marie, the horse, was harnessed to a sled. The sled was going up the hill to collect the sap. There were large pails on it. The children all scrambled up for the ride, even Jacques, the Jolicoeur baby of two. George let Peter hold the reins. There wasn't much to do because the horse knew her business and trudged mechanically up the hill behind the house, along well-worn tracks. She wore a collar of bells, which tinkled as she went. She had to stop every so often. Then the children swarmed off the sled and collected the little pails from the trees. They poured the sap into the big pails on the sled, jumped on again and, gee up! on they went.

On top of the hill there was a big container. The Mitchell children helped the Jolicoeurs to lift the full pails from the sled and empty them into the big container. From there the sap flowed through pipes into the sugaring house.

It was Timmy's turn now to hold the reins, as they rode in the sled along the many tracks, winding among the trunks of the maple trees, sniffing the pure tingling spring air, hearing the tune of the first songbirds, and feeling the sun warm on their hands and faces.

When they had collected enough sap, Ste.-Marie was allowed to rest, with a blanket over her perspiring body, while the children tramped through the snow to the sugaring house. They could sniff the sweet smell from afar.

Smoke and steam came from a shed which had a chimney sticking out of it. When the children entered the shed, they found it filled with steam. You could hardly see. There were stacks of wood at one end, and every now and then Mr. Jolicoeur would open the furnace door and shove in more wood. The furnace was much longer than the kind of stove you cook food on. It took up almost the whole of the shed. Peter and Timmy walked around it to see how it worked. It was really only a huge pan on legs, with a fire under it.

Outside there was another fire, under a little tank with a chimney of its own. Some sap was boiling there too. That was the sap they were going to eat. The other guests whom the Jolicoeurs had invited were standing about in groups. The grownups talked; the children played around. The sun threw checkered patterns on the snow. Peter and Patsy watched out for Pierre, but he hadn't come yet.

"When do you expect him?" they asked George. But George shrugged his shoulders.

Maman Jolicoeur presided over the outside tank. It was giving forth a good smell and the children hung about it like bees. Maman took a long-handled dipper and filled it with the brown, bubbling syrup, which she poured in generous quantities on the snow. There it cooled and mingled with the snow crystals into a new and delightful kind of candy. The children found clean white chips of wood on the ground, left after a tree had been chopped down. They scooped up the maple taffy with these, as soon as it was hard enough, and began to munch it. The Mitchell children had never tasted anything like it—it wasn't too sweet; the snow made it airy, cold, and crisp. It melted joyfully in your mouth, caressing your tongue and all the way down your throat with the golden taste of maple.

Mrs. Jolicoeur smiled a happy smile. She stood among the trees, looking grand and powerful. She seemed to belong there, as if she were a part of the earth and the good things that grow on it. Plump with her own good cooking, she was the picture of health and good nature. You could think of worlds coming and worlds going but Mrs. Jolicoeur standing there forever, a ladle in her hand.

Mr. Jolicoeur was quite different. He was small and wiry with a leathery brown face, creased into many wrinkles. It was easy for him to smile; the grooves were already there. He spoke in a lively way, and instead of looking permanent, he gave the impression, on the contrary, that he might fly off at any moment.

At first, everybody concentrated on the maple candy. There seemed no end to the syrup that came out of the little tank. Ladle after ladle was dipped into it and the contents spread on the snow. At last the snow all around the shed was polka-dotted with brown spots. The children scooped and licked and munched. Their faces and hands were getting sticky, but there was plenty of melting snow to wash with.

After a while the sugar did not go down so easily any more. Still, it was hard to resist those fragrant little pools of golden syrup. Angela was heard to sigh. "I don't know *what* is worse—to want to go on eating, and no more candy, or to have lots of candy and not be able to eat any more!"

Still Pierre hadn't come. The Jolicoeur children were getting anxious now too. " 'Ee will miss all the fun," said Aline to Patsy, with a compassionate expression.

"Let's play hide and seek," proposed Peter.

He felt like getting rid of some of the energy he had stored up. The others fell in with that, except the very small ones, who of course were being kept safely near the grownups. George was "it" and started to count, "*Un . . . deux . . . trois . . . quatre . . .*"

Angela wandered farther than the others, looking for a hiding place. At first she had tried to team up with Madeleine, but Madeleine was inseparable from Noel, and also rather childish, thought Angela. She did nothing but giggle. So Angela wandered off by herself, sniffing the pure mountain air. She felt like a bird let out of a cage, with the fields and woods and mountains all around her, the wide mantle of the sky above her and not a wall or a pavement in sight. Angela liked being alone. It made her feel part of the stillness around. The whiteness of the snow seemed to enter into her, making her feel clean and happy. She looked for a place to hide, but when she found one there always seemed a better one ahead. She wandered farther and farther. In the distance she could hear the shouts of the other children.

She went up the hill where the tracks of the sled plowed the snow. There were fewer trees here and more patches of sunlight. It was very still. Somewhere she heard the panting of a wood saw. She went on, longing to see what was on the other side of the hill. Angela remembered how Grannie had always loved a *view*. Would there be a view on the other side? She found a trail and followed it. The trees began opening out and suddenly a panorama spread out before her, a glorious winter landscape of rolling snowy hills shaded with the delicate pencil strokes of leafless trees. Here and there she could see the dotted Morse signal of a fence, or the dark silhouettes of evergreens. In front of her the ground descended abruptly. It looked as if the hill had suddenly broken off. As Angela gazed down the precipice she saw rocky peaks

sticking through the snow and dwarfed trees clinging
desperately to the steep hill. It didn't look like a very
safe place, and Angela was just turning to go back when
she heard the mewing of a kitten. She stood still and
listened. Yes, there it was again, "Mew! Mew!" like a cry
for help. The sound came from below. Away down that
precipice there was a kitten in trouble. Angela couldn't
turn her back and leave that call unanswered.

She lowered herself carefully, watching for handholds
and footholds. The snow made everything slippery. Once
she almost fell, but she grabbed at a stout little pine tree
just in time. Her heart beat fast and her breath came in
choking gasps, but the kitten's cries sounded closer and
closer and that encouraged her.

Maybe God sent me here to save it, she thought. The
little creature sounded so pathetic. Slowly but surely Angela descended. Her dress got ripped on a rock, and the
snow came right inside her boots, melting down to her
feet, but she didn't care. Once she dropped into a sort of
gully and stood to her waist in snow; another time she fell
and rolled down until a tree stopped her, but then she was
already almost at the bottom. The kitten kept mewing
and mewing, telling her where to go. At last she found it.
Poor little beast, it was caught in a rabbit trap. Its paw was
held between the iron teeth of the trap, and it could not
get out.

"There, there," murmured Angela, feeling angry with
people who set out traps. How would they like to be
caught in the middle of nowhere, in great pain, and stay
out all night in freezing weather? If Angela ever became
very, very rich, she'd take care no one would be allowed
to trap animals any more. Maybe she'd have to buy all the

traps herself and destroy them, but that would be better than having an innocent little animal suffer.

She tugged at the trap, and the kitten lay still. It stopped mewing and looked at Angela with trusting blue eyes. It was a small yellow kitten with long, fluffy fur. Angela tried to find the spring that would open the trap. But she couldn't see it anywhere. She tried pressing at various knobs, she tugged at the jaws of the trap, she pushed, she pulled, but she could not open it. Poor little kitty! Its eyes pleaded with Angela. It even licked her hand with its sandpaper tongue. Angela looked around her. If only someone would come—a man, who knew about traps! But there was only silence all around, broken now and then by the falling of a blob of snow from the branch of a tree.

Perhaps she could lift trap and all, thought Angela. She shuddered at the idea of embracing that instrument of torture. She tried once more to open it, but without success. Something would have to be done. She could not leave the little animal in pain much longer. If she could bring it home, Daddy or Mr. Jolicoeur might be able to open the trap. Angela clenched her teeth and tried to lift the trap. It was half frozen to the ground and took a lot of tugging to loosen, but at last she had it. The kitten got scared and scratched her, but she managed to reassure it. The trap was heavy and she had to support the kitten properly, or its paw might hurt too much. Finally she found the least uncomfortable way to carry the heavy clumsy thing. Then she looked up at the precipice and a new thought struck her. How was she going to get back?

It was teatime. Mr. and Mrs. Jolicoeur and the other grownups had returned to the house. Mrs. Jolicoeur called the children in for tea. They came trooping from all directions, gay with exercise and fresh air.

Mrs. Jolicoeur fitted into the old kitchen as if it had grown up around her. As she was pouring out tea in thick china cups, her movements had a queenly grace. "*Asseyez-vous, asseyez-vous,*" she said to her guests with a generous motion of her hand, pointing out chairs and benches.

The kitchen was filling up with young people, who shed galoshes and scraped boots and scrambled for places. Suddenly there was a jolly tinkle of sleighbells and a gay voice calling outside.

"Pierre!" cried Maman Jolicoeur, putting down her teapot.

"Pierre!" cried Papa Jolicoeur, putting down his pipe.

"Pierre!" shouted the little Jolicoeurs, streaming out of the house.

When Pierre came in, laughing, he was beset by young brothers and sisters, all hanging on his arms and even his legs and as hard to shake off as puppies. The first thing the Mitchell children noticed about Pierre was that he had grown very tall, much taller than his father, and that his voice had become deeper. His face, which had always been handsome, was brown and rugged now, with strongly marked eyebrows and finely chiseled features. But his smile was as merry as ever, and his eyes had remained the kind, twinkling black eyes of the Pierre they had known so well. His dark hair still curled in the old way, a stray lock falling over his forehead. Pierre went up to kiss his mother and father, according to French custom, and then he shook hands with Daddy.

"How are you, Mr. Mitchell? I'm so pleased to see you."

"Congratulations, Pierre, my boy, on your prize. We're proud of you!"

"Oh, it was nothing," said Pierre modestly. "There were many other entries just as good as mine. But you do not know how grateful I am to you for introducing me to Monsieur Latour. It has made all the difference to my life."

The girls noticed that he spoke English fluently now, though still with a musical French accent.

"Why did you never look us up?" asked Daddy.

Pierre made a grimace. "All my days were as full as a meat pie," he said.

Daddy laughed. "I can well believe it."

Pierre noticed the Mitchell children and greeted them. Then his attention was claimed by his own family again. Peter and Patsy, who wanted to consult him about the statue, found it hard even to get near him.

Their chance came when Maman Jolicoeur brought out enormous platters of hot jam tarts, which soon had the children as quiet as mice. Pierre handed the tarts around, and as he offered the plate to Peter, Peter whispered to him, "Listen, I want to ask you something, but I don't want everyone to notice."

Pierre nodded to show that he had understood. "Come with me, Peter," he said. "I want to show you some of my things." He led Peter away to a corner where some of his carvings stood on a little table. "What is it?" he asked.

Peter told him about the fight and the broken statue.

"What should I do?" he asked anxiously. "Daddy can't pay a hundred dollars. Not at this moment, anyway, with the new twins—"

"Come to our shop in Montreal," said Pierre. "Monsieur Latour in Rue St. Jacques. He'll find something that's less than a hundred dollars, I'm sure. I'll ask him."

"Oh, *thank* you." Peter looked his gratitude, and Pierre smiled.

"You're a little taller, but still just the same," he said affectionately. "Patsy is the same too. Joan is a young lady now, eh? Timmy is still himself and Catherine is quite changed. But where is Angela?"

"Angela? Isn't she here?" Peter looked around. There were so many children milling around the kitchen that it was hard to distinguish a particular one. But as soon as Peter began calling, "Angela," everyone noticed that there was a brightness missing among all those fair and dark heads—the splash of Angela's curls!

"When did you see her last?" asked Daddy, grown anxious.

"We were playing hide and seek," said Patsy, her eyes wide with alarm. Angela was her special favorite.

"I saw her go up the hill," cried Timmy, his mouth full of tart. François confirmed this.

"She go up André's trail," he added.

"That's bad. That leads to a cliff—it's dangerous there. We'd better look," said Mr. Jolicoeur.

So Daddy and Mr. Jolicoeur, Pierre, Patsy, Peter, and Joan went to look for Angela. The others stayed at home, for too many would only make confusion, said Mrs. Jolicoeur.

With Mr. Jolicoeur there to show the way it wasn't hard to find Andre's trail, where fresh footprints encouraged them to go on. They called, "Angela! Angela!" but there was no answer. Arrived at the precipice they saw the wide landscape spread before them, washed in golden evening light, with long purple shadows streaking across the snow, and far away the hills melting in a mauve haze.

"Angela, Angela!" they cried.

"She has gone down here," said Pierre, who had been studying the footprints.

"Angela, Angela!"

No answer, only the caw of a lonely rook, flying back against the brilliant sky.

"I'm going down," said Pierre. He eased himself down the steep slope and soon they lost sight of him among the boulders and trees and shrubs. Daddy wanted to follow, but Mr. Jolicoeur said it was better to let Pierre go alone. It was a difficult climb, and there was no use wasting energy; they might still need it. They listened anxiously, hearing Pierre's footsteps receding into fainter and fainter sounds. Then they heard the glad hallo of his voice.

"I've found her!"

Again Mr. Jolicoeur restrained the others from rushing down to join Pierre. "You only make it harder for him to come back," he warned.

It seemed an age that they had to stand there and wait, while the scrambling noises became louder and louder and louder. And then Pierre emerged, half carrying a worn-out Angela, who was clasping a little kitten.

"All is well!" cried Pierre. "She was stuck on a ledge, couldn't get up and couldn't get down, and she is hoarse from calling."

Poor Angela! She snuggled gladly into her father's arms, unable to make more than a very soft, croaky sound with her voice. She had called for help so much and so long. She had managed to get halfway up the slope with the heavy trap in her arms, but then she had got herself into the position Pierre had described, where every move had seemed fatal. She had sat there for the past hour, with cramps in her limbs, trembling with fear and full of concern for the suffering kitten. Pierre had seemed to her like the angel Gabriel himself when he had swung into view and reached out his strong young arms to lift her out of her prison. He had opened the trap and released the kitten's paw, and after that, with Pierre's help, Angela had managed to climb the rest of the way up the cliff. The Mitchells heard the whole story later, for Angela could not talk at first.

It was a triumphant procession that walked back to the Jolicoeurs' house. Daddy carried Angela, her head on his shoulder and her hair falling down his back like golden rain.

When she saw the state Angela was in, Maman Jolicoeur immediately produced blankets and made Angela drink some warm wine. She also bandaged the poor kitten's bleeding paw.

"That kitty," she said, "belong to people who were here for Noël. They come to ski, and go away, leaving the *minou* behind. It young still, too small to look after itself, so I 'ave been feeding it. If you like, you may keep it."

If anything could have made Angela feel completely well again, that would have done it.

"Oh, *thank* you," she whispered, burying her face in the kitten's warm fur. The other Mitchell children were delighted too; most of all Catherine, who clamored for the kitten but had to be told that it must get better before she could fondle it.

It was late now and time for the Mitchells to go home. They had had a wonderful day, and they all thanked Mr. and Mrs. Jolicoeur warmly.

"*Au revoir! Au revoir!*" they cried.

Pierre accompanied them to their car. When Sweet Chariot moved off and the Mitchell children turned for a last glimpse of the Jolicoeur house, they saw Pierre still standing there, gazing after them.

SEVEN

Uncle Armand

THE next day was Sunday, and after early service, Daddy was trying to find a quiet spot to eat his breakfast and read the Sunday papers. Mother's room was no good; the babies were howling and Miss Thorpe was tidying up there. Timmy and Peter were quarreling in the kitchen over the use of the frying pan. The living room was littered with the comic sections of the newspaper, and Patsy was poring over them, noisily crunching an apple. Even Daddy's study was invaded; he found Angela there, weeping over her kitten.

"I'm afraid she is *dying* . . ." she sobbed. The poor little creature did seem to be suffering. Daddy examined its little paw; it was badly swollen, and the kitten felt hot to the touch.

"We'll take it to Uncle Armand," he decided, folding up his paper with a little sigh.

"Who is Uncle Armand?" asked Angela in a quavering voice, still slightly hoarse.

"Oh, Uncle Armand is a gentleman I know. He looked after our parrot, when he had pneumonia, don't you remember?"

No, Angela didn't remember.

"Well, he's a great old character; you'll like him. He lives not far from here, in a house he built himself. He has wonderful skill with animals; people bring their pets to him from all over Montreal."

"Oh . . ." There was a ray of hope in Angela's blue eyes.

"But it's Sunday," she remembered, her gloom returning.

"Uncle Armand won't mind. He is always at home and we can't let the kitten suffer till tomorrow! We'll go right away—but we must have something to eat first. Did you have any breakfast?"

"No, I forgot." Angela still looked peaked and listless after her adventure of the day before.

Daddy went to the kitchen and came back with apples and milk and two cheese sandwiches. "That's the best I could do," he said. They sat cosily together over this meal and Angela cheered up when the kitten licked some milk off her finger.

"She wouldn't eat before," she said. "Do you think Uncle Armand will cure her?"

"Yes. If you are ready, we'll go at once. It's no use phoning; he hasn't got a phone."

Angela felt proud to be walking alone with Daddy. It didn't often happen to her; she was the middle child and often got left out of special treats that fell to the oldest and the youngest. To be singled out like this was an exception. She snuggled her slender hand into Daddy's big one. Daddy was pleased too. He held her hand tight.

"Do we have to take the streetcar?" asked Angela.

"No, we can walk it."

Angela gave a little skip. She liked walking better. They went along the river, where the ice was breaking. They could hear its loud, cracking noises, like pistol shots. Soon the ships would be passing again, with their gay plumes of smoke.

Uncle Armand's house was a quarter-of-an-hour's walk away, and stood in an unbuilt-up field. The beginning of a new avenue petered out into a track, which led to a crudely built house among some shrubbery. It was just as well that it was away from other houses, for Angela noticed the barking of many dogs when they approached it. They had to open a gate in a wooden fence and pass some kennels before they came to the front door, which was painted a bright red. There was a sign over it, in English and French.

ARMAND TROTTIER. VETERINARY SURGEON. ANIMALS
TRAINED, BOARDED, AND GROOMED.

Daddy knocked at the door. It was opened by a stocky little man with a wooden leg. He had a red, pointed beard and he wore glasses.

"Ah, Monsieur Meetchell!" he exclaimed. "This ees a pleasure!"

"Bonjour, Uncle Armand," said Daddy, shaking his hand.

"This is Angela, my number three daughter. You have not met her yet."

"No, I've met only you and your wife—she came with the parrot last year, no?"

"Yes. Well, it's a kitten this time."

"She caught her paw in a trap," explained Angela, holding up the pathetic little patient.

Uncle Armand's blue eyes twinkled down at her. "Bring her in here," he said. Daddy and Angela followed him into his surgery, a little room at the end of the hall, where Uncle Armand examined the cat.

"Her leg is fractured," he said, "and she 'as an infection too. I'll set 'er leg first, and then I'll give 'er some antibiotics." Uncle Armand got busy with the kitten, while Angela watched with her heart in her eyes, suffering everything she imagined her pet must feel.

"Now we give 'er an injection," said Uncle Armand, when he had splinted and bandaged the leg, "and then she must rest a little." There was a tiny bed in his surgery, rather like a doll's crib, covered with wire. It had a soft mattress and Uncle Armand put the kitten on it, covering her up with a blanket.

"She'll be all right in half an hour," he said. "Come and 'ave a cup of cocoa with me while you wait."

"Oh, but you mustn't trouble yourself," protested Daddy. "We can go for a walk and come back when the kitten is ready."

"No, no," insisted Uncle Armand. "I like visitors. It is seldom I 'ave a man to talk with, always the ladies." Angela thought he didn't sound as if he were fond of ladies.

They followed Uncle Armand through a little kitchen into the living room. It reminded Angela of pictures she had seen in a book of Daddy's called *The Old Curiosity Shop*—it was so full of things. There were many clocks ticking away, birdcages hung from the ceiling, and the mantlepiece was cluttered with toys. On a worn horsehair sofa lay several cats. A boy was stretched full length on a rug with a little fox beside him. He jumped up when he saw the visitors and backed away.

"Don't go, Paul," said Uncle Armand. But Paul kept retreating until his eyes met Angela's. He stopped, and his scowl diminished.

"Hello," said Angela.

"Show Angela the animals outside," suggested Uncle Armand.

"All right." The boy still looked surly, but not unwilling. Angela, delighted at a chance to see more animals, joined him gladly. The little fox followed them outside.

"Come back for your cocoa," Uncle Armand called after them.

"You didn't have a boy here before, did you?" asked Daddy, sitting down on the chair that Uncle Armand held out to him after brushing a small white rabbit off it.

"No, he is my nephew," said Uncle Armand. "Queer t'ing—his father died when 'e was quite young, and 'e lived all the time with 'is mother, my sister. Then, three months ago, my sister, she marry again, a wealthy man from the States. Nothing wrong with 'im, wants to be a good papa to Paul. But Paul, 'e doesn't like it.

"They go to live in Boston, but Paul most unkind to Stepfather. My sister, she cry. 'What must I do?' she say to me. 'I took 'im to the doctor and the doctor say it's a mother complex.'

" 'Give 'im to me,' I say. 'Maybe I can cure nephews as well as animals.' No good keeping 'im in Boston while 'e feel like that. 'E must get over 'is feelings, that takes time, no? It was a shock, you can imagine. Live ten years without a papa and suddenly there is a brand-new one. I can understand it. So 'e is 'ere now till 'e asks to go to Boston of 'imself."

"That is very good of you," said Daddy.

"Oh, me, I like children," said Uncle Armand. "Paul and I, we are good friends, and 'e is good wit' animals."

Uncle Armand poured four cups of cocoa from a kettle on the small coal stove. As if they had smelled it, the children came in, looking cheerful and relaxed. Angela was fondling the fox and chattering about the animals she had seen, while Paul chimed in with bits of information. They flopped unselfconsciously on the floor and began drinking their cocoa.

"How can you take care of so many pets, Uncle Armand?" Angela asked.

"I like it," said Uncle Armand, stroking his stubby red beard. "I rather work with animals than with people, they more easy to please. Children easy to please too," he added with a smile. He pointed to the toys on the mantelpiece. "I made those."

Angela got up to admire the tiny dogs and cats, the little parrot, the rabbit, the lamb.

"You're clever," she said. "We know a boy who can do that too—Pierre Jolicoeur."

"*Tiens*, you know 'im?" Uncle Armand was delighted. " 'E works for Monsieur Latour now. Monsieur Latour says 'e very good. I work for Monsieur Latour once, but I don't like making saints. Never see any. I see animals all the time. Monsieur Latour not like animals. So we part." He took up a piece of wood that was lying on the table and began to whittle at it with a pocketknife.

"I always like wood," he remarked. "Modern tings are made with steel and tin, 'ard, sharp, cold tings wit'out smell. Or worse, there are tings of plastic, spineless gooey stuff wit'out character. Wood 'as personality; it is alive, warm, fragrant . . ."

"It's got splinters," said Daddy smiling.

"At least you can't make bullets of it," countered Uncle Armand. "I know wood, 'ow it grows. I was a logger when I was young, before I lost my leg."

Angela looked at his wooden leg. "How did you lose it?" she asked.

Uncle Armand peered at her over his spectacles. "This bear did it," he said, stamping on the bear skin which was spread in front of the stove. "Finish your cocoa and I tell you about it. It 'appen up at the logging camp. A she bear was prowling around it till we dared not leave the fire. One of the men—'e 'ad been to the States and knew everythink—'e said, 'Why don't we shoot 'er?' 'Shoot a bear in winter?' we all said. 'That's bad luck.'

" 'I don't believe it,' said the man 'oo 'ad been to the States and knew everythink. 'I am going to shoot 'er.' We all shake our 'eads, but when a man 'as been to the States, what can you do? And sure enough it was bad luck all right. The bullets missed and the man 'oo 'ad been to the States only saved 'is life by climbing a tree.

" 'Just what I told you,' I said to 'im, as 'e sneaked back to the camp. 'You catch more bears with honey than with bullets.'

" 'I don't believe it,' 'e says.

" 'Watch and see,' I say, and I split a log and wedged it up. Then I put a nice lick of 'oney inside the split. The bear was 'ungry. Soon she was sticking 'er 'ead in the split, trying to get the 'oney out of the tree. 'Pull out the wedge!' shouts the man 'oo had been to the States. I did pull, but it stuck.

" 'Elp me!' I cried.

"The two of us pull and push and meanwhile the bear finishes the 'oney and starts on my leg. I pull and pull, but by the time the wedge is out, the bear is out too and my leg is in.

" 'Ha ha,' says the man 'oo had been to the States, and 'e shot the bear."

"So it was good luck for you, after all," said Angela, but she looked rather sad about the bear.

"No—we cook the bear and the man 'oo 'ad been to the States got the piece with the bullet in it and choked on it. Bad luck for 'im! And my leg no good any more, so not very good luck for me either, and the bear dead, so no luck for 'er."

"Why was it so bad for the man to have been to the United States?" asked Angela. "We were born there." To her surprise she heard an exclamation from Paul. He had jumped up as if he'd been stung.

"You're a *Yankee!*" he cried. "Why didn't you tell me?" And he ran out of the room, slamming the door.

Angela looked shocked. "What's the matter?" she asked. "What's wrong with being American?"

"Never you mind," said Uncle Armand, getting up to answer a knock at the door. " 'E is upset because 'e 'as an American stepfather. That's all."

The knock proved to be another customer, an imperious old lady dressed in furs, who wanted to board out her shivering little lapdog.

"Liver every day," she commanded, "and a bed of his own, and a bath every week." Uncle Armand agreed solemnly with it all. She was about to depart when she swerved suddenly and cried, "*Fleas!* You have other dogs—they have fleas?"

"Not a flea in the 'ouse, Madame," Uncle Armand assured her gravely. "I 'ave special method. I 'ave decoy."

He sounded very mysterious and the lady asked with popping eyes, "What do you mean, 'decoy'?"

"I 'ave a special dog, most hattractive to fleas. 'E 'as been bred for the purpose. I keep 'im outside and if a flea came in 'ere, by error, it would 'op out to that dog, first chance it got."

"Poor dog," murmured the lady sentimentally, "he must be very uncomfortable."

"Ah, Madame," Uncle Armand assured her, "you forget, 'e was bred hespecially for it, chasing fleas is—'ow shall I say it?—'is *métier* . . . passion . . . life's work . . ."

"Ah, how clever," murmured the lady. She took a tender farewell of her Fifi and left, satisfied.

"Do you really have a special dog in the yard for fleas?" asked Angela, when the lady had gone.

Uncle Armand winked at her. "Madame, she scared of imaginary fleas," he said. "So I 'ave bred imaginary dog to take care of them."

He went to his surgery to inspect the little patient. "I think she'll do now," he said, putting the kitten in Angela's arms. The kitten stretched her free paws and yawned, as if she'd been waked out of a delicious sleep.

"Well, thanks a lot, Uncle Armand," said Daddy, taking leave. "We've had a delightful morning! About the patient—you'll send me a bill, won't you?"

"I ham very businesslike," Uncle Armand assured them with twinkling eyes. "Come again; it is so refreshing to 'ave customers not worried about fleas!"

Daddy was still chuckling when they were walking home. "Grand fellow," he muttered.

"But, Daddy," remarked Angela, "he said that he wanted to talk with a man, and he was talking himself all the time."

Daddy was amused that Angela had noticed this. "My dear," he said, "as you grow up you'll discover that what people want is not people who'll talk to them, but people who'll *listen*."

Angela had to think that over.

"Why does Paul not like Americans?" she asked, after a profound silence in which father and daughter had pursued their own thoughts. "Isn't it queer?"

"No," explained Daddy, "it's not so queer, really. He was happy alone with his mother and now a strange American gentleman has taken her away from him. So he feels he hates all Americans. It's wrong, of course, but our feelings do not always go the way they should."

"But, Daddy," said Angela, "we didn't take away his mother—we've never even *met* her!"

"No, you're right, my dear. It is unreasonable. Feelings are not always logical. We have to watch out for that and argue with ourselves. Paul is too young to do that. I think his mother's marriage came too suddenly."

Angela sighed. "He was so nice when he thought I was a Canadian," she said. "I liked him then. Do you think he'll ever change?"

"I hope so," said Daddy. "Feelings don't last forever, you know. They are the most changeable thing about people."

"Perhaps we can still be friends then," said Angela hopefully. She looked down at the kitten. It was purring for the first time since Angela had known it.

"I don't think she is in pain any more!" Angela cried joyfully.

When they reached Friendly Gables, they were greeted by Timmy and Peter, who cried, "Oh, Angela, there you are! We were looking for you. We're going to show Joan Homework after lunch. Mommy has given us money for a party!"

Daddy wondered what was so exciting about homework, but he was anxious to get back to his weekend papers, so he did not inquire further.

The others had worked all morning in the attic to prepare for their party. When the moment arrived, Joan was blindfolded. At first she giggled a bit, but Peter told her sternly that she would have to keep very quiet or she would not be allowed to go, and that made her serious immediately. So she was led up the ladder and conducted to their den. There Peter took her bandage off.

Joan looked around and an exclamation of delight escaped her. The children had kept adding to their treasures and improving their hide-out until it had become the coziest place in the world. The sun was streaming through the little window, which Patsy had washed and which now had little net curtains. Angela's dolls' house stood underneath it, and the little rocking chair she had got at Christmas. Behind the couch they had hung an old curtain and they had pinned some gay magazine pictures on a screen they had found. There was an old stable lantern with a candle in it on the bookcase which they had made of orange crates. Most of Peter's and Patsy's books had landed there. Some of the boys' pennants hung on the wall above the window and Timmy's soldiers paraded on the trunk. A few model airplanes dangled on strings from the rafters and their collection of bows and arrows hung against the wall they had made of boxes.

The children had filched several footstools that had only seemed in the way downstairs, and with the sofa and the mended chair that made plenty of seats. The chair had been decorated for Joan with pink paper roses. A card table was spread with a clean cloth. On it stood Mother's treat: raisins, doughnuts, and apple juice in paper cups.

Joan said it was absolutely wonderful. "How did you keep it a secret?" she asked jealously. "Oh, *there's* where my trash basket went! I was looking for it everywhere. And Jules Verne's books—no wonder they weren't in their usual place! Oh, what fun! I'm glad I belong here too now. I love it here."

"Yes, it's cozy, isn't it?" said Peter proudly. He had tilted up the electric heater so they could feel the heat on their hands. But actually it wasn't very cold any more. They could hear the drip! drip! of melting snow outside.

They started on the food, and Angela told what she had been doing that morning. (She hadn't said much at lunchtime because of Miss Thorpe.) Peter was so interested that he forgot to eat.

"That must be *my* Paul," he cried. "Has he dark hair and does he blink his eyes a lot, and do his nostrils quiver like a horse's?"

"What do you mean, *your* Paul?" asked Angela.

"Oh, just a boy in my school," said Peter, wondering whether to say more. "Shall I tell them?" he asked Patsy.

"Why not?" said Patsy. "They may be able to help and they won't tell Mommy."

"No, of course not," said Angela. "What is it, Peter?"

So Peter told the story of the fight and the broken statue. They were all much concerned and wondered what to do to help.

"What a horrible boy," said Joan.

"No, he is not horrible, really." Angela defended him. "He was quite nice at first. You know, Uncle Armand's dogs all like him and he has a little fox he has tamed himself. He found it as a cub. I don't think animals would like a *bad* boy," she ended thoughtfully. The others laughed.

"If you want to get into Angela's good books, you've got to have a reference from an animal," said Joan.

"But why does he act so mean then?" asked Timmy.

Peter frowned. "I can understand it in a way," he said. "You know how we all feel about Miss Thorpe. Yet we know she'll go away soon. She isn't our stepmother."

"No, that's true." The children sat in awed silence. Fancy having someone like Miss Thorpe for a stepmother!

"But Daddy says Paul's stepfather is nice," Angela pointed out. "He wants Paul, only Paul doesn't want him."

"Maybe he does not *really* want Paul," said Timmy sagaciously. "Maybe he is just pretending."

"Still, I think Paul should go home," said Joan. "I don't think it is very kind to his mother to behave the way he does."

"Daddy says people can't always help the way they feel," announced Angela.

"Why doesn't he go home and build himself a Homework?" asked Timmy.

"I think Uncle Armand is his Homework," said Angela. The other children nodded.

"Ours is better, though," said Timmy.

"But we don't hate all English people because of Miss Thorpe!" protested Peter.

"I think it's only because of Eunice and Mr. Spencer— and the Bastables—that we don't," said Patsy. "If Miss Thorpe was the only English person we knew, we might hate them all."

The others agreed, remembering Mr. Spencer and his granddaughter Eunice, English friends of theirs whom they had known in Washington, before the Spencers had moved to London and the Mitchells to Montreal.

"Then Paul ought to meet some *nice* Americans," suggested Peter.

"Aren't *we* nice?" asked Angela.

"Well, he hasn't properly met us yet," said Peter.

"Why don't we invite him here?" proposed Patsy. "Let's write him a letter and tell him we understand about his trouble and ask him to visit us? We could have a party up here!"

That was a wonderful plan. Peter sneaked down to find notepaper and a ballpoint pen. Unfortunately he was waylaid by Miss Thorpe, who wanted him to hold up a skein of wool she was winding. Peter was too polite to refuse, but he stood gnashing his teeth with such agony on his face that Miss Thorpe let him go again, though she called him a selfish boy. This seemed grossly unfair to Peter, and it was with a heart full of sympathy for Paul that he returned to Homework.

Now they had to compose the letter. Joan would write it—anyone could read her writing; it was so neat.

"Dear Paul," she put down. "We heard from Angela this morning why you do not like Americans. We—" She bit her pencil. "What next?" she asked.

"We have a nurse called Miss Thorpe," continued Patsy. "She is English and she would make us hate all the English if we didn't know some nice English people."

There was a moment's silence. What now?

Timmy said, "We are nice Americans." But Angela thought that sounded boastful and they all agreed they couldn't very well say it.

"We thought perhaps you don't know many Americans," Peter went on. "So would you like to visit us?"

"He'll never come," objected Angela. "He ran away when he heard I was a 'Yankee,' as he called it."

"And he *hates* me," Peter remembered.

"Well, we'll tell him we have a secret," said Patsy. "That ought to fetch him."

"Tell him we have a dog," proposed Angela.

"Tell him it's a *shipwrecked* dog," added Timmy.

That sounded good, so Joan wrote:

"We have a secret meeting place and we have a dog who was shipwrecked in the last war and found on a raft by our father." Another full stop. What next?

"He may think it is an ambush," said Peter, worrying. "After all, I'm his enemy."

"Say: 'This is fair and square, cross my heart and hope to die,' " shouted Timmy.

So Joan wrote it down.

"Say: 'We are really your friends, though you don't know it,' " added Angela.

"And we must all sign it," said Joan, handing the paper and pen around. Timmy signed last, in crooked print.

"Wait," said Angela, "I want to write a P.S." And she wrote: "**WE HATE STEPFATHERS TOO.**"

EIGHT

The Statue

JOAN had been struggling with herself ever since she had heard of Peter's problem. She knew Daddy and Mother couldn't afford any extra expense at present. Miss Thorpe was staying on longer than had been originally planned, because of Mother's slow recovery. As the eldest, Joan knew more about her mother's and father's financial worries than the others did, and to ask Daddy to replace the broken statue at this moment was out of the question.

But where was the money to come from, then? The

children talked about earning, but how much earning could they do in three weeks? Even if Joan herself went baby-sitting (and she had no time for that now) she wouldn't manage to earn more than a few dollars at the most. Peter had mentioned that Pierre might help. But Pierre couldn't do miracles. Joan could see no other way out than to offer her dress money. If it had just been the money, she would not have minded. But it was the dreams, too, that she had to offer. No use thinking about going to a dance if she didn't have a dress! It would take her ages to earn all that money over again—she might be an old maid of eighteen before she finally got to a dance! It was a hard struggle, and Joan hadn't quite decided the next morning, when Peter got a letter.

Joan was carrying a tray with Mother's breakfast on it. Miss Thorpe had asked her to bring it up, since Angela seemed too busy with her pussy although the kitten was doing very well. She noticed Peter and Patsy reading the letter in the hall.

"May I see it?" she asked. "Who is it from?"

Letters to the children weren't plentiful in the Mitchell household.

"It's from Pierre," said Peter. "Here, take it."

Joan sat down on the stairs and read:

"Dear Peter, I have mentioned your problem to Monsieur Latour. He says there are some old-fashioned statues in his cellar which he will let you have cheap. Why don't you come and look at them tomorrow (Tuesday), after school? I'll be watching out for you. Pierre."

"Oh, that *is* nice," cried Joan, a flush spreading on her

cheeks. "Do you think I could go with you, Peter? We could take the four o'clock train."

"I want to go too," said Patsy.

"Well, let's all three go—"

"And how will we explain that to Mommy?" asked Peter.

"We'll say we're going to look at Pierre's shop," said Joan. "She'll understand that. We've just told her about Pierre and his wonderful work! But we'll have to bring money."

"I have five dollars," said Patsy.

"I've two," added Peter shamefacedly.

"Well, I'll bring my money," said Joan, deciding her private battle with a bang.

"Oh, but Joan—your *dress!*" cried Patsy.

"It can't be helped," said Joan. Somehow the idea of visiting Pierre's shop had cheered her. She picked up the tray and carried it to Mother, but the breakfast had got stone cold.

"Mommy," said Joan, "Peter and Patsy and I want to go and visit Pierre's shop after school. He has invited us!"

"That's a lovely idea," said Mother.

But here Miss Thorpe intervened. "Very lovely," she snapped, "and who decided to do the supper in the evening? Who wanted to help with the babies? What's going to happen if the three eldest leave at the most crucial time of the day? Do you expect me to do everything? Already I've been washing dishes and rinsing undies and sweeping floors. It's not my job, but I do it when I see it can't be helped. Only if it means I'm helping a lot of lazy children to fritter away their time, I refuse. What kind of a girl are you, anyway—letting your mother's breakfast grow cold?

When I was young my mother meant more to me than anything else in the world. I'd have gone through fire for her, and she was strict with us. There wasn't all this sympathy with how we 'felt.' She taught us a sense of duty. I know the novelty of helping with the babies and doing the supper has worn off. But that's the time you should grit your teeth and stick it out, not give in."

Joan listened in stunned surprise to this outburst of Miss Thorpe's. She realized that her wish to see Pierre's shop had blinded her to the situation. Of course she could not leave. She told Miss Thorpe so. "But the others can go, can't they?" she asked anxiously. "I wouldn't like to have Pierre disappointed." She couldn't, of course, mention the serious reason behind this trip.

Miss Thorpe conceded that the others wouldn't be particularly missed. She seemed embarrassed at what she had said; she avoided looking at Mother. Mother knew very well that Miss Thorpe disapproved of her educational methods, but she didn't look crushed. She sat serenely munching her cold toast.

Miss Thorpe went downstairs in a ruffled temper and spread an atmosphere of gloom which set the children quarreling and made Daddy leave for his office much earlier than was necessary.

Peter arranged with Patsy that they would meet at the station in time to catch the four o'clock train to Montreal. Patsy had their combined money (twenty-seven dollars) in a purse of Joan's.

The weather that day was very bad. There was a bitter wind and it was snowing again. In Montreal it was even worse than in Lachine, as the high buildings created drafts. At the street corners the wind buffeted you with

such force that you were blinded and almost swept off
your feet.

Patsy literally couldn't see, as the snow had caked on
her glasses. She had to take them off. Peter warned her to
put them in her pocket, or she'd lose them.

They found the shop after some wandering about and
asking. It was cozily warm there. Pierre had been looking
for them and greeted them cordially. So did Monsieur
Latour, a short square man with a black mustache and long
black hair combed into his neck. He was inclined to stop
and chat, but Peter explained that they did not have much
time and wanted to see the statues. So Monsieur Latour
took them down to the cellar, which was full of gesticulat-
ing plaster figures, all gaudily painted, with much gold
ornament.

"They were in the store when I bought it," Monsieur
Latour explained. "Mass-production stuff. Done to make
money. What we French call 'Saint Sulpice,' because
there is a street in Paris of that name where they sell such
tings. But they're not for Henri Latour, oh no. I sell good
statues, made of wood, not plaster. Wood carving is an
old craft in Quebec. We must keep it up. But people here
will not pay for the good work. They prefer the cheap
statues. Do you know," he said, turning to Patsy, as Peter
was obviously bored, "that most of my customers come
from the States? There they appreciate good work. They
'ave asked me to open a shop there, but I love my own
country. I want to stay 'ere, and maybe people will wake
up and appreciate their own art one day."

The children were getting restive. They had to take
the six o'clock train back. Monsieur Latour noticed their
impatience and said, "Well, 'ere is a Saint Joseph for you.

A nice big one with glass eyes." He gave a little shudder. "You can 'ave it for thirty dollars, which is less than it cost me."

Peter and Patsy were delighted. It was a huge statue, even bigger than the one Peter had broken, with a glittering golden halo around its head and a bunch of lilies in its hand.

"But we have only twenty-seven dollars," said Patsy nervously, emptying her purse.

"Very well, twenty-seven dollars then," agreed Monsieur Latour amiably. "You'd better pay upstairs. I 'ave my cash register there."

Upstairs they met Pierre again. He wanted to know if they had found something.

"They are taking the big Joseph," said Monsieur Latour. "Where do you want it delivered?"

Peter gave the address of his school. He sighed happily. That was a big load off his heart. There was still some time left to see the shop, and all Pierre's carvings. Pierre showed them his studio, a little room behind the shop, where he had his modeling stand, his wood-carving tools, and an easel.

"I do portraits, to practice for the saints' faces," he said, showing a portfolio full of clever drawings.

"How long does it take you?" asked Patsy, smiling at a caricature of Monsieur Latour, which seemed all mustache and hair.

"Oh, not long. Sit down and let me make a sketch of you—without glasses. I'm not used to them yet; you didn't have them in Sainte-Félice. I like you better without them. Anyway, you've lovely eyes."

While Pierre was talking he moved his pencil rapidly

over a large sheet of paper, and Patsy appeared there under his hand, a dreamy Patsy, with velvety dark eyes under a tumble of soft curls, a large, generous mouth, slightly smiling at the corners, and a wide, sensible forehead.

Patsy was delighted. "Is that really me?" she asked

"Yes, it's very like you," Peter declared.

"Oh—but—it's *pretty!*" cried Patsy. "I'm not pretty, am I?"

"Not pretty, perhaps," said Pierre. "But I think you'll be beautiful one day."

"Oh!" Patsy blushed a deep rose and gave Pierre a look which made him smile.

"You can keep the drawing," he said.

"Oh thanks! Have you a paper to wrap it in?" Patsy practically danced, she was so pleased. She had always thought that her looks were hopeless, and here was an *artist* who told her that she might be beautiful. He ought to know!

Peter had been looking at the clock. "It's half past five," he cried. "We have to run!"

Patsy grabbed her coat and her precious drawing and they hurried out of the shop, after hasty farewells and fervent thanks. There wouldn't be another train till eight, and they had return tickets, so they could not go by bus.

They had struggled for some time against the wind when Patsy gasped, "My glasses! They aren't in my pocket—I must have dropped them!"

It was hopeless to look in the snow for them, and, besides, there was no time. They barely managed to catch the train.

Patsy was upset. She could only see a hand's breadth in

112   *Friendly Gables*

front of her, she was so used to her glasses, and what was she to do in school tomorrow? Besides, glasses were expensive. Where had she lost them?

"Put an advertisement in the paper," suggested Peter.

But Patsy shook her head. "If I've dropped them in the street they'll be useless now," she said. "They'll be trampled to bits."

It was bad luck. Patsy thought she still had an old pair but no matter how much she searched in drawers and cupboards she could not find them, so she had to go to school the next morning without glasses. It was especially awkward because the sale of raffle tickets had to be speeded up. The teachers had been grumbling that not enough money had come in for the celebration of the fête next week. Patsy had hardly sold any yet. Madame Garneau, their neighbor, had taken one from her (under protest), the mailman and the milkman had each bought one, and Daddy had bought five. Miss Thorpe had bought one too. But Patsy had lots of tickets left over. She started offering them in the streetcar (there people couldn't run away from you), and later during the lunch break, she teamed up with another girl and went up and down the streets selling tickets. Patsy really disliked doing it. She hated to bother people when they were going about their own business. But the teacher had sounded so desperate when she had urged the girls to step up the sales.

Jeanne, her companion, had taken the left side of the street. Patsy was taking the right side. She could not see people's faces properly, which was awkward. They seemed just blurs, but people were kind to her anyway and bought many tickets.

She approached a fat lady in a long black coat. "Would you like to buy a raffle ticket for Monsieur le Curé's fête?" she asked. "They are ten cents each, and you can win a lovely embroidered tablecloth." The woman seemed to hesitate.

"It's just so we can surprise Monsieur le Curé," Patsy added encouragingly. The woman dug her hand in her pocket and handed Patsy a dime. Patsy tore off a ticket from her book, which the woman took.

"I thought I'd told the sisters I didn't like all these raffles—" "she" said in a familiar masculine voice, as "she" stalked off.

Patsy blinked and stared. That wasn't—it *wasn't*—but it was! Jeanne came running to Patsy from the other end of the street.

"You idiot," she cried, "that was Monsieur le Curé himself! And he was mad . . . didn't you see his face?"

Alas, Patsy had not been able to see his face.

"Wee-ell," Jeanne whistled. "You've about spoiled everything for all of us! He has gone straight to the school to complain. He hates raffles! He'll probably tell the Sisters that he doesn't want a fête, and they've been working so hard preparing for it—enjoying their secret. Phew, I wouldn't like to be in *your* shoes today!"

Patsy went to the classroom on trembling limbs. She couldn't pay attention to her lessons and was scolded several times. It wasn't just that she didn't have her glasses; she couldn't keep her mind on what was going on. She kept wondering when the awful truth would be revealed, and what terrible doom hung over her.

Presently there was a knock at the door and her teacher was called out of the room. When she came back she looked very grave.

"There is a girl here," she said in sepulchral tones, "who has had the coarseness, the lack of refined feelings, to offer a raffle ticket to *Monsieur le Curé* for his *own fête*." A shudder went through the classroom. "Our secret is r-r-ruined," said Sister Marie Rose, "and Monsieur le Curé is very annoyed." There was a tremor in her voice. Patsy could have whipped herself. What a terrible thing to do to those poor Sisters. She noticed many children looking at her. She supposed Jeanne had been talking. There was a dreadful silence, during which no one spoke. Patsy wondered whether the teacher expected her to come forward and confess, in front of the whole class? She hoped not.

The teacher's natural gaiety was gone. The lessons went on, but in a subdued manner. Patsy was fighting her tears all the time.

Later, when the other children had left the classroom, Patsy went up to Sister Marie Rose.

"Patsee, how could you do it?" said the teacher, with such reproach in her voice that Patsy couldn't keep her tears in check any more. "If you wanted to sell a ticket so badly, why did not you buy it yourself?" the teacher asked.

"It wasn't that . . . I lost my glasses!" wailed Patsy, "and I thought he was a *lady!*"

The teacher smiled, half against her will. "It can't be helped," she said. "It was very unfortunate. I do understand now, but I don't think Sister Elaine will forgive you as easily as I do. I'm afraid that she has told me she won't let you sing in the choir any more."

Patsy felt that it was a mild punishment. She deserved much worse for spoiling everybody's fun.

Of course she was late again leaving school that day; Joan and Angela had both gone. Patsy longed for her mother's sympathy, but she realized that she could not tell her what had happened. Mother would want to buy her new glasses right away, whether she could afford it or not, and Patsy was still hoping to find the old pair.

She went rummaging again in drawers and cupboards as soon as she got home, but she had to go mostly by the feel of things, and Peter, realizing her difficulty, came to her aid. They didn't find the glasses, but the drawers were lined with old newspapers and Peter noticed that one of them had the story of Pierre's award in it. There was even a picture of Pierre beside the winning statue. Patsy could see it when she held it so close that it almost touched her nose. She said she couldn't recognize Pierre very well but all the same she wondered how they could have missed it before.

She ran to show it to Joan, who was in the kitchen, preparing supper.

"Let me see," Joan said, grabbing the paper. "That picture isn't like him, he's much handsomer." She read: "Promising young sculptor—remarkable talent . . . great plastic expression . . . will go far."

"We must keep this," she said, and cut it out of the paper with the kitchen scissors. Then she put it into her pocket.

"I like that," protested Patsy. "Peter and I found it!"

"Yes, but I am going to keep it," said Joan calmly. "You have the drawing." Joan had felt rather envious when Patsy had come home with her portrait done by Pierre. She had felt a little ache, thinking that if she had gone, she might have been the one Pierre had drawn.

"That's true," admitted Patsy, who guessed how Joan felt.

There was a ring at the door.

"Who could *that* be?" said Joan. "It isn't the wash, that

came ages ago—and it can't be a visitor, just before supper . . ."

But it was a visitor—a tall handsome young man with
merry black eyes, who grinned at Patsy when she opened
the door, and held out a pair of glasses to her.

"My glasses!" cried Patsy, putting them on. "Pierre!"
she gasped. "How did *you* get them?"

"You left them in my studio," he explained. "You took
them off when I drew you, don't you remember?"

"Oh, *thank* you for br-bringing them," stammered Patsy.
"You've no idea what a time I've had without them."

"I can imagine," said Pierre, laughing.

"Please do come in," urged Joan, who had followed
Patsy. "Have supper with us, will you? It's almost ready—
sauerkraut and frankfurters."

"I love sauerkraut and frankfurters," Pierre admitted.
"But isn't it too much trouble?"

"Not at all, we'd *love* to have you. Let me take your
coat. What a clever picture you did of Patsy," Joan went
on. "We all admired it very much. It's just like her."

"Would you like me to do one of you?" Pierre asked
eagerly. "I've got pencils and paper with me, and it's still
light."

"I'd love it." Joan laughed delightedly. "Patsy, could
you finish supper for me?"

"Oh, sure," said Patsy, feeling powerful with her glasses
on.

Pierre seemed all animation. "Where can you sit?" he
asked. Joan led him into the living room.

Pierre took some time posing her. He looked at her
from every angle with his eyes half closed. Joan began to
feel embarrassed. At last Pierre was satisfied. He put his
drawing pad on his knee and began to sketch rapidly.

"You're quite different from Patsy," he said.

"Oh?" murmured Joan. She was trying to sit as still as possible.

"Yes. You've got classic features, Patsy's are irregular. You will *always* be beautiful, no matter what happens, but Patsy's beauty will depend on her expression."

He said it so coolly that it didn't sound like a compliment but Joan's heart beat faster all the same.

They were interrupted by Timmy's bursting into the room with the triumphant announcement that he had earned *fifty cents* shoveling snow. "Oh, hullo!" he said when he saw Pierre.

"Hullo," said Pierre, without looking up from his work. "What are you going to do with the fifty cents?"

"It's for Felicity," said Timmy, running off to put it in his savings bank.

"And who is Felicity?" asked Pierre.

Joan smiled. Pierre hastily erased a few lines and tried to put in the smile.

"She is Timmy's girl," Joan said. "We've never seen her. Timmy won't bring her here, because he says we're not grand enough. She must be a sort of queen, according to Timmy's descriptions. She certainly rules over his heart. Every penny he gets he saves to buy her a golden bicycle, and he saves his sweets for her too. I even found a forgotten lump of maple sugar in his pocket yesterday. He'd saved it for Felicity the day we were at your place, and he wouldn't believe that it was really too dirty to give her, poor fellow."

It was getting dark, and Pierre said he thought he'd have to stop. "I don't think it's a success," he said. The drawing was more worked out than the one of Patsy, and it hadn't the same sure lines. But it did portray a very lovely Joan, gently smiling. Pierre had caught the serious look in her eyes and the sensitive curve of her mouth. Joan was deeply pleased.

"May I keep it?" she begged.

Pierre hesitated. It was obvious that he wanted it himself. "All right," he said. "But let me do a better one of you some time, eh?"

They heard Daddy come in, and Joan ran to show him the drawing. Daddy was pleased with it. He shook Pierre's hand.

"Well, well," he said, "I see I'll have to commission you to do a head of my wife one of these days. We can't have you spoiling us with free pictures all the time."

Patsy announced that supper was ready. Joan felt sorry that she hadn't chosen more romantic food, but Pierre saw nothing wrong with it and ate heartily. It was a happy meal. Daddy made jokes, and even Miss Thorpe looked pleased. Art was one of the things she approved of, and Pierre was very polite and respectful to her. They had a long conversation on British painters. Miss Thorpe admired the older paintings, which had a story to them, and Pierre tried to tell her that the story was not the important thing—it was the way you arranged colors and shapes that was important. Afterward Miss Thorpe told Joan that she thought Pierre a very intelligent boy.

Meanwhile the children were longing for supper to be over. They wanted to take Pierre up to Homework. They dragged him off as soon as they could, swearing him to secrecy. Mother called to them from her room and they had to go in to her for a moment. Pierre was rather shy at first but Mother soon put him at his ease. Joan showed her Pierre's drawing and she liked it very much, though she said she preferred the one of Patsy.

"Yes, you're right," agreed Pierre. "Patsy's is a better work of art." Pierre had a peek at the twins, who were getting quite fat, and then the children pulled him out of the room.

Pierre was mystified when they took him into a closet. Nowadays they always closed the door first, and then took the ladder from a hiding place and put it up.

They had begun to do that because Miss Thorpe had been wondering where they disappeared to all the time. They had seen her snooping about, peeking into closets, so they knew that if she saw the ladder she'd be sure to find out. Peter had also taken to locking the door, leaving the key under his pillow. But they didn't bother to do that every time: a locked door was too conspicuous in the Mitchell household.

Of course Pierre was too grand to be blindfolded. But it was almost more fun to see his gasp of astonishment when he walked through the dirty, dusty attic and suddenly came upon their paradise. It had benefited greatly by the fact that Joan had joined their company. Joan was a better cleaner than the others and she had more sense of order. Also, she had managed to wheedle some things out of Mother. She had made a kind of sideboard out of a packing case and brought up an electric kettle. They could make tea now, or instant chocolate, or even consommé with bouillon cubes. That was very *real*. She had also brought up two armchairs which she said no one would miss downstairs. They had enlarged their den a little to take in the new furniture, and it was beginning to look really elegant with a second rug: a motheaten hearthrug Mother had said they could have.

"It's the best room in the house," declared Timmy proudly, throwing himself on the couch.

"It is magnificent," agreed Pierre, who was young enough to enter into the spirit of the thing, especially when Joan told him it was a fortification against Miss Thorpe.

"Poor Miss Thorpe," he said. "She has had a hard time with you. You do not seem to have appreciated her."

"No, we certainly don't!" cried the children, but his words made Patsy reflect that perhaps there was another side to that question.

Pierre regretfully remarked that he would have to go. He had to go back to Montreal, where he lived with Monsieur Latour and his wife. The children felt sorry. They tried to make him stay longer. But he told them that Madame Latour would be nervous if he came home too late.

When he had taken leave of Daddy and Miss Thorpe, the children escorted him to the door and waved after him, crowding in the doorway to watch him stride off, a tall silhouette under a canopy of stars.

Afterward, in the girls' bedroom, Joan sat brushing her hair. She brushed it longer than usual. Patsy had already rolled herself into a ball when Joan asked, "Do you like Pierre?"

"Of course," murmured Patsy. "I've always liked him. I think he is clever and he is *fun!*"

"Yes, isn't he?" sighed Joan, and went off into a dream.

NINE

Paul

THE new statue was a success. Peter was called to the headmaster's study when it arrived, and Monsieur Leger thanked him personally.

"It's very like the one you broke; how did you find it?" he asked curiously. "I don't believe the man who gave it will notice the difference."

In the classroom the statue was admired too. Peter felt proud of it. Every time he looked at it he felt happy. But he was worried that it might be broken again. He warned the other boys not to walk too close to it.

During recess Paul came to him. Paul had not spoken to him after the accident. He had seemed sullen. He had not even mentioned the letter. But now he went up to Peter and said in a husky voice, "T'ank you for not telling on me." He noticed Peter's surprised glance and blushed. "You see, I would 'ave 'ated to ask my new father for the money. Uncle Armand, 'ee 'as not much money. But I know I should 'ave paid too, you understand?" He looked anxiously at Peter.

Peter nodded, embarrassed. He still thought that Paul had acted in a cowardly way, but he was willing to make allowances. Paul added shyly, looking at the ground, "That letter—you mean it?"

"Of course we meant it," said Peter. "You never answered."

"No." Paul looked uncomfortable. "But I would like to veeseet," he said.

"Well, of course. Come tomorrow, after school."

That evening there was great excitement in the Mitchells' house. The phone rang, and Daddy went to answer it but came back with an amused smile on his face.

"It's for my eldest daughter," he said.

Joan jumped up. "For me?" She didn't often receive phone calls.

There was a deep masculine voice at the other end of the line. "Hullo, Joan, this is Pierre," it said.

Joan gave a gasp. "Pierre, hello, how are you . . ."

"I'm fine. We're having our annual Beaux Arts ball next week and I was wondering whether you'd like to come with me."

"*A Ball!*" Joan nearly dropped the phone. "Wait a moment, while I ask Daddy—" She ran into the living room, her eyes blazing blue fire.

"Daddy," she panted, "Pierre says he wants me to go to the Beaux Arts ball with him next week! May I—please—may I, Daddy?"

Daddy looked a little dubious for a moment. A Beaux Arts ball sounded rather grown-up for Joan, but Pierre was a dependable boy and Daddy didn't want to quench the light in Joan's eyes, so he said, "All right, then."

Miss Thorpe muttered that in England girls of fifteen weren't allowed to go to dances.

"Well, we're not in England," Daddy told her drily.

Joan had accepted jubilantly, and Pierre had hung up, before she remembered that she had no dress.

She burst into Mother's room with the news. "Pierre has asked me to go to the Beaux Arts ball—and Daddy says I may go!"

"Oh, child, how delightful for you!" Mother said happily. "Your first dance!"

"But, Mommy, I've no dress."

"I thought you were saving up for one?"

"Yes, Mommy, but—" Joan hesitated. Still there was really no reason to keep the accident with the statue a secret any longer, now it had been so beautifully solved. So Joan told Mother the whole story, and Mother listened spellbound, fascinated by the way the children had taken care of their own problem.

"May I tell this to Miss Thorpe?" she asked. "It may make her understand my children a little better."

"As long as she doesn't let the other children know that she knows," said Joan. "I don't think they'd like it."

"Well, let's discuss your difficulty. Let me think—I suppose I haven't anything you could alter?"

Joan shook her head. Poor Mother, she never wore anything glamorous . . . and this dress had to be perfect.

"I like your navy-blue silk," began Mother. "If you lengthened it—"

"Mommy, this isn't a *hop*," said Joan. "It's a *ball*." Mother had to admit that she hadn't realized the grandeur of a ball. Her teens had been spent in the depression, when no one had money for balls.

"We must think of something," she said, frowning. "Perhaps Miss Thorpe will have an idea."

But Joan said she didn't think Miss Thorpe approved of her going to the dance.

Joan discussed the matter with Patsy later in the bedroom. Patsy could not help much either. All Patsy's dresses were too narrow and too young. But she did have a fan which Grannie had given her, of carved ivory, a treasured possession. She offered that.

"Oh, thank you," said Joan. "I'll be careful of it."

"Can't you make your own dress?" asked Patsy. "I know girls in school who do it, and you're so clever at sewing, Joan. *I*'d be hopeless, of course."

"That's an idea . . ." said Joan slowly. "I could get some simple material, that wasn't expensive—Mommy would be able to pay for that—and a nice pattern . . ." She was already making the dress in her mind.

The next day, after school, Peter brought Paul home with him. Unluckily that was just the day when Miss Thorpe had finally lost patience over the kitchen floor. She hadn't been able to get any of the children to clean it. They promised, of course, but did not do it. Angela was still absorbed in the rapidly mending kitten. Joan was all excited over her ball and had already started on her dress. Miss Thorpe pinched her lips into a thin line when she thought of it. Ridiculous nonsense, letting a girl go to a dance when she should be concentrating on her homework, and on helping Mother. Weren't the twins excitement enough for any girl? Miss Thorpe shook her head. People were too soft with their children in this country.

Meanwhile the kitchen floor had got so dirty that Miss Thorpe had mopped it herself. And just as she was surveying the result with a certain amount of pride, in burst Peter and Paul, through the back door. Peter was so intent on showing Paul his home, that he forgot to take off his galoshes. Paul did not think of his, either. The streets were muddy with melting snow and a considerable amount of it soon spotted the clean floor.

"Will you children *ever* think of anyone but yourselves!" Miss Thorpe scolded. "Can't you *see* this floor has just been washed? What kind of behavior is that?"

It embarrassed Peter. What would his friend think? He drew Paul into the back porch and they silently took off their galoshes. Then they sneaked through the kitchen, where Miss Thorpe was repairing the damage they'd done, hoping she would say no more. But she did. Their ears rang with her complaints.

"Don't mind her," whispered Peter when they were safely in the hall. "She is the English woman we told you about."

"Oh," Paul nodded in complete understanding.

Trusty jumped up at them, wagging his tail. "This is the dog we wrote you about," said Peter.

Paul patted Trusty, who looked pleased. Catherine came tripping out of the living room, her hair neatly brushed by Miss Thorpe, and her face clean. Her eyes had a solemn, disapproving expression.

"Peter!" she cried. "Joan can't use the *pink*ing shears on blue stuff, *can* she?"

Those were feminine mysteries that did not concern

Peter. "Come here, Catherine," he said. "This is Paul, say hullo. It's my youngest sister, Catherine," he told Paul.

"She wasn't in the letter," said Paul, puzzled.

"No, she can't write yet."

Joan called to them from the living room. She had some light-blue dotted Swiss material spread on the floor and was cutting out a pattern. The floor was littered with pins, scraps of materials, and papers. When Joan saw Paul she jumped up.

"The others are expecting you upstairs," she said with a friendly smile. "I'll come too. Catherine, go ask Miss Thorpe to give you a cooky: she's in the kitchen." Catherine trotted off, and Joan explained to Paul, "We had to get rid of her. We're taking you to our secret place, and she's too small."

As Paul followed Joan and Peter upstairs, he felt a thrill of anticipation. He had never really played with other children. At school there were just sports and fighting. He had never been allowed to bring friends home; his mother had thought it too much trouble. When she was struggling to keep up a job as well as rear her son, the extra wear and tear of hospitality would have finished her. But it had made a lonely child of Paul, and it had kept him too dependent on his mother. It had also made it difficult for him to understand other children. He'd been impressed by the fact that Peter had not told the teachers about his part in breaking the statue. He knew he would not have been so honorable himself. The Mitchells' letter had pleased him, too, though he hadn't known how to answer it. He had reread it often and had formed a picture in his mind of a houseful of children, where even the dog was romantic and there were secret meeting places. His enthusiasm had been slightly dampened by Miss Thorpe's reception, but now that he was about to be shown the hiding place, his heart bounded.

For the children the mystery surrounding Homework had become more or less routine. They had grown to love the place apart from its secrecy, as a joint creation of their own. But to Paul it was the last word in romantic excitement to be shut in a dark closet, shown a ladder by flashlight, and told to mount into a dusty garret, meanwhile being warned not to make a sound.

The garret inspired him with fear; he seemed to see spiders leering at him from the cobwebs which hung from the rafters. But then a curtain was pushed aside and he entered the children's sanctuary.

The electric heater shed a glow. Timmy was lying on the floor on his stomach, writing a book in crude printed letters. He held his pencil tightly, as if he was afraid it would escape. Angela was playing with the kitten, who was getting much livelier, notwithstanding her splinted leg, and would grab with furry paws at a dangling string. When rolled up, she looked like a purr with fluff around it. Sometimes she licked herself with a tongue like a pink comma. Angela called her "Caramel" because of her color.

When they saw Paul the children jumped up. "Hurray, you came!" they cried.

"Hush," warned Peter. "Do you want everyone to hear?"

They settled themselves cosily around the electric fire.

"We thought you weren't coming," said Patsy, "when we didn't hear from you after our letter."

"Yes, why didn't you answer?" complained Timmy in an aggrieved tone. "We were looking and looking for your letter, we even asked the mailman, but he said there wasn't any."

"Well—" Paul found it hard to explain that the Mitchells hadn't seemed quite real, not people you wrote letters to, only people to think about. He now realized that he had committed a breach of etiquette. "I'm sorry," he said. "I'm very glad to be here." He looked around the homemade little room with its odd collection of objects and gave a wriggle of delight.

"I'm going downstairs to get some food," whispered Timmy.

"Be careful Miss Thorpe doesn't see you; she is on the warpath," warned Peter.

When Timmy returned, with a bottle of milk and a box of gingersnaps, he looked mysterious.

"I just managed to grab them while she was putting the diaper can out in front, for the man to collect," he whispered. "I think she saw me going upstairs and I'm sure she is looking for me. We'll have to be quiet." They listened for a while.

"Did you pull up the ladder?" asked Joan.

"No, I was afraid it would make too much noise." Timmy looked anxious.

"Perhaps we'd better haul in the ladder all the same," said Peter. "We'll do it very quietly, because otherwise, if she looks in the closet—"

They waited for a moment, debating what to do. There was a noise of footsteps on the second-floor landing. They could hear Miss Thorpe's voice in the hall. She was saying, in an annoyed way, "Where *did* they all go to? Catherine, you tell me. They are not doing their homework at all, I don't see them anywhere. Someone's got to look after you while I bathe the babies. What's got into Joan? She's no help any more."

Joan was blushing. "I forgot Catherine," she whispered. "I'd better go down. There's the supper too. I've a pie in the oven . . ."

"Wait, it's too dangerous now," warned Peter.

They heard Catherine wail, "I wanna go to Mommy!" Then they heard a door open and shut. There was a silence.

"Miss Thorpe has taken Catherine into Mommy's room. I'd better slip down now," whispered Joan.

When she was gone the others explained to Paul the difficulties of keeping their secret.

"There's Trusty too," said Angela. "Sometimes he sees us disappear and starts scratching at the closet door. Then one of us has to go down and lock him into the boys' room."

"If I were Miss Thorpe I'd have found out long ago," boasted Peter.

"Perhaps she's so glad to get rid of us that she does not like to find out," suggested Patsy.

"Except when she wants us," gloomed Timmy. "She is always wanting *me*. Even when I'm *terribly* busy shoveling snow for Felicity, she wants me to come home."

"Who is Felicity?" asked Paul.

"Oh, she is a girl I'm friends with," said Timmy. "I'm buying her a golden bicycle, but it takes a long time." He sighed. "I earned fifty cents, but now it's melting again."

"What? The fifty cents?" asked Peter.

"No, the snow, of course!"

Patsy had poured out milk and was dealing out gingersnaps. They began munching cozily.

"Do you know what I'd like?" said Peter dreamily. "I'd like to dig a secret underground tunnel, with different outlets. No enemy could ever find me. They'd pursue me, and I'd run away; they'd be close on my heels, and suddenly, presto, I'd be gone. They'd stare, and stare, but they wouldn't be able to find me, because I'd have escaped through one of my hatches."

"Dig the tunnel to my house," proposed Paul. "Then we can visit each other secretly."

"Yes, and I'd put food on the shelves," said Angela. "And blankets, and books. Then we could stay there a long time."

"We'd need a flashlight," said Timmy.

"No, lamps, or it would be too scary," Angela pointed out.

"Who'd dig a long, long tunnel like that?" asked Patsy.

"Oh, we'd have trained animals," said Angela.

"Yes, Uncle Armand would lend them to us," agreed Paul, who enjoyed this fantasy and had already pictured to himself a daily trip to the Mitchells via this fascinating underground passage.

They heard the closet door open downstairs and they wondered whether it was Joan coming up. There were heavy steps on the ladder. It didn't sound like Joan at all . . . was it Miss Thorpe? The children had jumped up and were looking at one another with alarmed eyes.

Peter ventured to peep through the curtain and saw a head emerging. "It's *Daddy!*" he cried.

Yes. It was Daddy, all six feet of him. He was laughing.

"I heard suspicious noises," he said, "and I thought, before I buy rat poison, I'd better have a look at what size they are. So this is where you've been hiding, is it?"

The children were all tugging at his arms and pulling

him into their sanctuary. "Oh, Daddy, come and look what we've made!"

"Well!" He sank down on the sofa. "This *is* cozy, I must say. A heater and all! And here's Paul, too. Hullo, Paul! Well, well. I hope you don't mind your father's having found out your secret, do you?"

"Oh no, Daddy, we like it—as long as you're not angry. Have a cooky."

"And spoil my appetite for supper?" asked Daddy. But he took one all the same. "Yes," he said. "I was home early from the office, and I saw no family. So I went in search of them, and here I find they've made themselves a refuge to hide away from their old father!"

"Oh no, no, Daddy," the children protested. "Not from you, we like *you* here. We're hiding from Miss Thorpe."

"Miss Thorpe?" Daddy looked as if he were terribly surprised, but the children knew he was acting. "Miss Thorpe is a most remarkable and most capable and most kind woman. I'm surprised you want to hide from her."

"Well, she doesn't make *you* wash your hands every minute," complained Timmy.

"And she doesn't ask *you* to hold up knitting wool," said Peter.

"And she doesn't worry *you* about duty all the time," added Patsy.

Daddy made a comical grimace, rubbing the back of his head. "I'm not sure you're right," he said. "I think she disapproves of me too."

"Oh, Daddy, how could she!" The children were indignant.

"Yes, she thinks I'm a weak parent. I can see it in her eyes every time she looks at me. That's the trouble with very good people," said Daddy, stretching himself out on the sofa and relaxing with a sigh. "They make lesser people feel uncomfortable."

"That's our guilty conscience, I suppose," said Patsy.

The children had gathered around their father. Timmy was searching in his pockets for chocolates. Angela was leaning against him on the other side. She had deposited Caramel on his lap and he was stroking her. Peter and Patsy sat on the floor, at Daddy's feet, looking up at him with glad faces on which the electric fire shed a rosy glow. Paul was watching the group with a wistful expression.

"Really," said Daddy, "I wish I'd discovered this paradise of yours sooner. It would have saved me some rather dull evenings. It's much nicer here than downstairs."

Before Paul left he was taken into Mother's room, as Mother had asked to see him. She naturally wanted to meet the boy who had caused such turmoil in her son's life. She gave Paul a warm smile, but he was most interested in the twins and kept standing by the cradle, gazing at them. He breathed a deep sigh.

"I wish I 'ad brothers and sisters," he said.

"Perhaps you will have, now your mother has married again," Mother pointed out. Paul's head jerked up and he looked at Mother with startled eyes.

"I never thought of that." He flushed, and his eyes began to shine. "Big families 'ave fun, 'aven't they?" he said meditatively. "I was always alone."

The Mitchell children escorted Paul to the door, but before he left he turned and asked Peter longingly if he might come again. Afterward the children danced around with glee.

"We're making Paul fond of Americans!" they chanted.

TEN

Changes

BECAUSE of her blunder about the raffle ticket, Patsy was more or less ostracized at school. She had sunk in the estimation of her teachers and fellow students, or, to put it more simply, they were all mad at her. Patsy felt it, but she could understand it. It was her own stupid fault. Why couldn't she be more careful, more tidy, and punctual?

Patsy admired the generous way in which Joan had parted with her dress money. Patsy alone, of all the family, had an idea of what that had cost Joan. She felt that she had misjudged Joan a lot, and she resolved to be more like her and to help her more with the housework.

So Patsy began to straighten out the turtle hole after she got up in the morning. She folded up her clothes and put her books in the bookcase. There were no more disemboweled chests of drawers.

But Joan was undergoing a different sort of transformation. Fits of dreaminess overcame her, in which she sat staring in front of her, doing nothing. The tidiness of her part of the room was relaxing. She spent a lot of time in front of the mirror, fixing her hair in new ways, and bobby pins and curlers would be left astray on her dressing table. She also took to doing her nails, causing the room to smell of nail polish. She took her sewing to bed with her, which meant threads on the floor and pins scattered about. As a result the room ceased to have a divided look. It became one room, all of a sudden.

The school feast of Monsieur le Curé was approaching and Patsy felt very sorry to have no part in it. Joan and Angela were both singing in the choir. Joan was already fixing up their best blouses for it. Joan sang well; she sang alto and was one of the choir's main supports. Patsy had a nice voice too, but as she was a soprano she would not be missed; there were too many of them.

Patsy was fond of Monsieur le Curé. He had always been kind to her and whenever she had good marks in catechism he would smile at her and give her a picture of a French saint. The last time she'd got Ste. Genevieve. It had the story printed on the back of it of how Ste. Genevieve had saved Paris.

Patsy wanted to show Monsieur le Curé that she, too, rejoiced at his fête. So she made a poem.

The candles grow like yellow flowers;
  The organ sings.
    The children sit in rows, all dressed in black,
      Huddled like birds upon a tree,
        Huddled together against eternity,
          And with their thoughts make incense in the air.
      The curé stands in prayer,
        Blessing us with his heart's embrace
        And with God's love upon his face.

She decorated it with pictures of Monsieur le Curé, the candles, and the birds. She showed it to Mother, who liked it very much.

"Do you think Monsieur le Curé will like it? It's not too silly?" asked Patsy anxiously. "I couldn't find the proper rhymes for the beginning."

"That doesn't matter," said Mother. "It's much better that you said what you wanted, instead of changing it to something else just because it rhymed."

"Yes, but it would have been better poetry," said Patsy, "if it had rhymed all the way."

She put the poem in an envelope and dropped it into Monsieur le Curé's mailbox with the following letter:

Dear Monsieur le Curé:
    I am sorry I sold you a raffle ticket by mistake—it was because I had lost my glasses. I'll never do it again. The Sisters were very angry with me because they all wanted so much to surprise you. So I won't be able to sing for you in the choir. I didn't want not to do anything for your feast day so I made you this poem. It's not very good, but you see I'm not very practiced in making poetry. I am sorry it is not in French. I hope you are not angry any more because of the raffle tickets.
                    Sincerely yours,
                    Patricia Mitchell

The snow had definitely melted now. It had melted so much that the Mitchells' cellar had flooded and to Miss Thorpe's horror the children started a naval battle there on floating barrels, with broomsticks. Poor Catherine tumbled into the water and had to be hauled out by Peter. Miss Thorpe said she'd never seen such goings on and they were all sure to get pneumonia, but they didn't even catch cold.

As soon as the sidewalks were clear of snow, in the third week of Miss Thorpe's stay, tricycles and roller skates appeared everywhere. Timmy did not have roller skates, but he begged the loan of Peter's.

"I'll have to make them smaller," grumbled Peter. "Won't it do some other time?"

"No," explained Timmy. "You see, Felicity has roller skates, and when I bring her home after school, I have to run all the way." Peter agreed that that was undignified and let Timmy have his skates.

Timmy's fund for the golden bicycle was not getting on very fast.

The whole family had let him polish their shoes for a penny each, and Miss Thorpe had had hers done twice. But shoveling snow was finished, and what else is there for a little boy to do?

Meanwhile Timmy's friendship with Felicity had reached a climax—she had invited him to tea.

The whole neighborhood rang with his shouts of "Good news" when he came to announce this stupendous piece of luck. Of course he could not go to her empty-handed, and he did not like diminishing the bicycle fund. So he decided to finish the book he had started a while ago. He had sewn some leaves together and was printing a story on its unequal pages. It was a story the teacher had told in class. Timmy wished to immortalize it in this way. Occasionally he'd asked the others for the spelling of a word, but sometimes he'd just guessed—it was quicker. After he had finished printing the story, he decorated it with lovely crayon pictures of flowers.

He felt very proud of the result and showed it to his parents, to Miss Thorpe, to the girls, and to Peter. They all praised him for it. Catherine liked it so much, she wanted to keep it. Even Miss Thorpe said it wasn't bad for a boy not yet seven. She didn't think an English boy could have done better, which was high praise from her.

This is what Timmy had printed, in rather higgledy-piggledy letters of different colors:

Once upon a time there was an ant an a cricit. The ant was greedy but not cricit o no no! The ant was storing away for the winter, but the cricit was singing all summer.

He had no food when winter had to come. So he went to the ant for some food. It was cold so it took him a long time to get to the only ant he knew. The cricit went up to the door and he said: "Can I have some food please?" And the ant said: "No— you can get it yourself, you Brat" and the cricit went with nothing. He went through all that trouble for nothing. But if the ant came to the cricits house to get some food, the cricit would have given him some.

On the cover of the booklet Timmy had printed:

THE STORY OF THE CRICIT—IN CASE, TIMMY

"What do you mean—'in case, Timmy'?" asked Mother.
"Well, in case you want to know who wrote it," answered Timmy.

On the day of the party the whole Mitchell family was involved in seeing Timmy off. Joan had to sponge and press his Sunday suit, while he watched critically to see that she didn't skip a spot. Peter had to lend him his best tie (Timmy had used his as a leash for Trusty), Daddy's hair-oil bottle was practically emptied on Timmy's hair, and Patsy had to tell him on which side the parting looked best. Miss Thorpe lent him one of her own handkerchiefs, and Angela gave him her pink soap to wash his hands with.

The family waved him off, as he marched proudly away, looking like a boy out of an advertisement, with Felicity's present, done up in white tissue paper, clutched under his arm.

But when he came back he did not cry, "Good news!" He sneaked quietly into the house. No one even knew he was home. When he appeared at the supper table the others all looked at him in surprise.

"Back again, Timmy? What happened?"

Timmy glowered at his plate. His mind was crowded with pictures: An elegant lady, smelling of roses, who had said, "So you're my little girl's sweetheart!" A big room, opening onto a sun porch where a teaparty had been prepared, with tiny cups and plates and dolls sprawling around on chairs. Felicity bossing him . . . saying, "No, you mayn't sit there—your place is next to the teddy bear. . . . You can have only *one* cake." And Felicity hadn't even looked at his story—the grownups had taken it and had *laughed* at it; he had heard them. But how could he tell all that?

"It was a silly party," he growled. He brooded for a moment. Then the indignation which had accumulated in him during the afternoon burst forth. "Felicity is just a *girl!* That's *all!*"

There was a hush around the supper table. The whole Mitchell family felt as if a familiar star which had gladdened them for a long time with its radiance had suddenly dropped out of the sky with a hiss. Farewell, Felicity.

But Joan had cooked a delicious meat pie and hot rolls, and there was ice cream for dessert. Timmy cheered visibly, and at the end of the meal he gave a satisfied sigh and said, "Now I don't have to worry about a golden bicycle any more."

The household was beginning to relax a bit. Mother seemed much better; she was able to get up and walk about on the second floor. Daddy had given her a new bathrobe of deep red which looked very well on her. The children began to run to her again with every little thing. Nobody forbade them any more. Miss Thorpe was still there, helping with the babies, preparing Mother's trays, but she was less formidable.

That meant that they also began to pay less attention to her. It was as if they felt that she had already gone, as if she had become a ghost. Peter even said to her one day, when he entered the kitchen after school, and found her there, "I don't suppose you'll be staying very much longer, will you?"

"I'm not gone yet," she answered, "and take your cap off when you come into the house; that's good manners."

Another time, when Catherine in an exuberant mood called her "Thorpy," she slapped the child's hand.

She seemed to be getting more irritable while everyone else was getting less so. Angela called it "Miss Thorpe's ruffled nerves."

It was Patsy who found out the reason. She chanced to go into the living room one afternoon when Miss Thorpe was dusting there. Miss Thorpe didn't notice her, for Patsy had come in very quietly. And then Patsy saw that Miss Thorpe was weeping. She kept sniffing and blowing her nose. Her eyes were red.

Patsy stood aghast. That Miss Thorpe could feel un-happy had never occurred to her. For a moment she stood quite still and imagined that she was Miss Thorpe, going to work for the Mitchells. Would she have liked it? Or would she have noticed that they all hated her? Her heart brimmed over with sympathy, and impulsively she went to Miss Thorpe and kissed her.

"I'm sorry we've been so beastly to you," she said.

Miss Thorpe was startled. Then she burst into sobs. It was just as if the sobs had lain there waiting for a long time, and now they came tripping over each other.

Patsy put her arm around Miss Thorpe and said, "There, there," the way Mother always did. When Miss Thorpe quieted down after a while, Patsy said, "Do you feel better now?" just like Mother, and Miss Thorpe smiled.

Then she began to speak. It wasn't at all what Patsy had thought. She wasn't crying because the Mitchell chil-dren had been so horrid to her, but because she had to go away. She said she'd got so interested in them and so fond of them, she couldn't bear to leave them. Patsy was too amazed to know what to say. She would never, *never* have guessed that Miss Thorpe loved them. And then Miss Thorpe began to say such nice things—how amusing Timmy was, and how she doted on Catherine.

"Nobody could ever be bored in your house," she said with a little sob. "It's always interesting, even when everything goes wrong. I know you don't like me, that was not to be expected, since I had to take your mother's place. But I'll miss you so much."

Patsy thought this was the most splendid thing she had ever heard—that someone could love people when she knew they did not love her back. It was magnanimous and Patsy didn't think she could have done it.

"I like you," she said impulsively, feeling that if she hadn't had time to yet, it was bound to come. "And I'll help you when Joan is dreaming. Joan thinks of the ball all the time, you know."

Yes, Miss Thorpe had understood that! She was smiling again. Patsy told her she should take a rest now. Patsy would go to Mother and help with the babies. Miss Thorpe said gratefully that perhaps she *would* go up to her room and lie down for a little while.

Patsy went to Mother's room. "I've sent Miss Thorpe to bed," she told her. "Do you know what? She was *crying* because she has to leave us! *Imagine!*"

Mother smiled. "Yes, Miss Thorpe is a dear," she said. "I'll miss her, too."

"May I wash the babies for you?" asked Patsy. "Joan is sewing her dress in Homework."

"Of course," said Mother. Though Patsy wasn't as skillful as Joan, she found that she had a soothing effect on the babies. They seemed happy when she handled them with her gentle, sensitive hands, and they didn't squirm or cry, as they did with Miss Thorpe. But Patsy *did* spill the water and drop the powder box and put on the babies' nighties back to front. When she finally had everything straightened out, a lot of time had elapsed.

"I'm sorry I'm so useless," she apologized with quivering lips, as she stood by her mother's bed.

"Don't say that, darling." Mother took one of Patsy's hands and pressed it. "You've a great gift."

"I?" Patsy stared. "I'm good at nothing. I make mistakes, I drop things, I'm clumsy, I'm lazy, I'm untidy— what gift have *I* got?"

"You have the gift of sympathy," said Mother. "It makes up for a lot of your faults and will be a comfort to many people."

When Patsy told the other children in Homework that Miss Thorpe had cried because she was leaving soon, they were all very surprised and sorry for her.

"Let's give a party up here," proposed Angela. "We can do it when she is almost gone, and it doesn't matter any more about our secret."

"Then we must have a present for her," said Peter. "And we've no money left."

"Yes, I've got a dollar." said Timmy.

"That won't be enough, but perhaps Daddy will help us," Joan said hopefully.

Paul's whistle sounded outside and they knew he was coming up. He came almost every day now. Sometimes he brought his fox, or some other pet from Uncle Armand's store. This time he carried a white mouse.

"Take care, Caramel may hurt him," warned Angela, but to everyone's astonishment Caramel didn't hurt the white mouse at all. She took it between her paws and started licking it, as if it were a kitten. The mouse was not a bit afraid of her either. It ran all over her. Finally it went to sleep between the cat's front paws.

"Perhaps they're too young to know they're enemies," said Patsy.

Besides the mouse, Paul had brought news. His stepfather was coming for a visit.

"Isn't that *awful?*" he asked, hoping for sympathy, but he didn't get any.

"I think it's very nice of your stepfather to take all that trouble about you," said Patsy. "Perhaps he really does love you. We've found out that Miss Thorpe loves us."

"No!" Paul was astonished. "How do you know?" he asked.

"Well, she cried because she's leaving us," said Peter in a flattered voice. Paul scratched his head thoughtfully.

"It makes us like her too," the others told him.

"Well . . ."

"Maybe you'll get to like your stepfather," suggested Patsy.

"Oh, 'e's better than Miss Thorpe," admitted Paul.

"Well, there now, you may get to like him very much!" the children cried encouragingly.

When Paul had to go he found the kitten and the white mouse curled up together and fast asleep.

"I'll leave 'im 'ere," said Paul. " 'Is name is Custard."

"Caramel and Custard," Timmy cried. "They belong together!"

ELEVEN

Festivities

THE festival for Monsieur le Curé was a success after all—and it brought unexpected honor to Patsy. She was sitting unobserved among the audience beside the boys, Miss Thorpe, and Daddy, who were all watching the performance. Joan and Angela were both looking their very best. Angela was in the junior choir and sang a song about the spring. You could hear her voice high above the others, see her face sweetly solemn under the halo of her fair hair. Joan's choir sang a more ambitious French composition in harmony. The long school auditorium was decorated with pine branches, which gave out a Christmasy smell (it was too early for flowers yet).

The Sisters presented Monsieur le Curé with a beautiful new gold fountain pen. He thanked them in French, and then said, "I have another present which I got by mail and I like it very much. I will read it to you." And to Patsy's amazement he read her poem to the audience. His accent made it sound prettier. Then he said in English, "That is a beautiful little poem. I shall keep this always, in memory of a little girl whose eyes don't see far, but verree deep."

Patsy swallowed a few times. Her eyes had misted over. Then she heard everyone clapping, and Monsieur le Curé said, "Come here, Patricia, and shake hands."

So she had to go forward and be stared at by everybody. When she went back to her place, she could see Sister Marie Rose beaming at her, but Sister Elaine looked sour.

"Did you see her face?" Joan whispered to Patsy afterward. "She was *furious*."

After Monsieur le Curé left, the Sisters raffled the tablecloth, and who should win it but Miss Thorpe!

She was tremendously pleased; her nose grew pink with excitement. The Mitchell girls felt proud that Miss Thorpe should have won a prize at their school. It was a magnificent tablecloth. Miss Thorpe bore it off triumphantly.

Joan had finished her dress, and everyone tried to compliment her, but it wasn't a success. It hung lumpily around her, hiding her pretty figure. Here and there it dragged and bunched. Joan kept ripping parts out and sewing them over. She and Patsy spent a lot of time over it but somehow the dress wouldn't hang right and the day of the dance was approaching.

"It can't be helped," sighed Joan. "It will have to do."

Paul had to give his criticism of the dress too. He had heard Peter and Angela say what a pity it was that Joan had to give all her dress money for the statue. Paul felt ashamed. For the first time he realized what a burden he had put on the Mitchell household by his behavior.

His stepfather's visit was turning out well, as the Mitchells had predicted. Paul found him quite nice and most generous. Paul realized that it was a wonderful thing to have a brand-new father of your own, and he began to tell him all the things that had happened.

In the afternoon before the dance Joan was frantically cleaning her evening slippers with benzine. She hoped they wouldn't smell too much. The dress was draped over a chair. Joan realized that the more time she spent sitting down the better. The dress looked all right when she was sitting. Unfortunately she just loved dancing.

There was a ring at the door. Someone brought in a big cardboard box, addressed to Joan. Joan undid the string with trembling fingers, while her brothers and sisters gathered around her. The first thing she saw when she opened the box was a note, lying on white tissue paper. "From Paul and his new papa," it said.

Then she drew away the paper and found the most beautiful formal evening gown you can possibly imagine: just the cornflower blue that suited her so well and that would go with her shoes. There is no describing the dress. It was the sort of dress every young girl dreams of. It had long, simple lines and yet romantic tucks and frills here and there, all in exquisite taste. The cut and fit were both perfect. When Joan put it on she looked like a queen. She couldn't tear herself away from the mirror. Even Daddy and the boys approved of her dress. Peter felt proud because it was he who had given Paul Joan's measurements. He'd guessed what was going to happen, but he hadn't let out a word.

Joan was so excited she had to go and lie down for a while. Patsy had taken over all her work. At eight o'clock, Pierre called for Joan, bringing a lovely corsage of creamy rosebuds. He looked extremely well in evening dress, with white gloves. When he saw Joan he gazed at her in admiration.

"You will be the prettiest girl there!" he exclaimed.

Joan was putting on Mother's fur evening wrap when she got a moment's panic. She didn't want to go. She was scared. She rushed up to Mother to kiss her, almost crying. But Mother understood. She said, "Don't worry, dear, everything will be all right," with such a calm, reassuring nod, that Joan got her courage back again.

The ball was given by the students of the art school, in a long room with a glittering dance floor. There were mirrors along the wall which reflected the lights and all the colorful dresses. Couples were pouring into the room, and others stood chatting. The girls wore lovely gowns and many of them had fans. Joan realized with a pang that she'd forgotten to bring Patsy's.

Pierre introduced her to some of his friends. One boy, who was called Gilles Mornay, had red hair standing up in a brush cut, a funny expression on his face, and an orange-slice grin, showing small teeth. The other boy was a little older and rather arty. He had dark hair which fell in a romantic sweep over his forehead, and he wore glasses with heavy black rims. His name was Hans Roda and he came from Eastern Europe. One of the girls was called Nella Gustovski. She was Polish and very attractive, with green, slanting eyes and copper-colored hair, brushed smoothly against her head.

The other girl, Stella Jones, was pink and placid with lots of make-up and artificially bleached hair. Joan did not like her much, but Stella was kind. She talked to Joan, trying to put her at her ease. Nella, whom Joan admired, took no notice of her.

There were tables with chairs around them along the walls. Pierre and his friends selected one and sat down.

And then came the terrible moment there always is at the beginning of a dance, the moment when the band began to play and the floor gleamed and everyone was secretly longing for a good time but outwardly pretending not to care. Nobody dared to make the first move. The music spilled away, wasted—time flew and no one stirred. Then, mysteriously, several couples took the plunge at the same time and swam out into the open. That was the signal. Soon the couples crowded one another and swirled along in thick congestion.

For Joan, of course, this was the great test. Would she be a Success? Were people going to like her? All the other girls seemed to be much more mature-looking, much more at ease, more striking in appearance. Timid glances at the mirrored walls showed Joan up as a pale insignificant person, not artistic-looking at all.

Pierre asked Joan to dance, and Joan found that he was an excellent dancer. She was glad that she had practiced her steps and could follow him. She had the next dance with Gilles. Gilles didn't really know how to dance but he was all for fun and didn't want to remain seated. So he had invented a rather complex step with a kick in it which was hard for Joan to follow. When she got in his way, he trod on her foot. She was glad when she could sit down again. Nella had been sitting the dance out with Hans. Joan again admired her rather blasé air. She was smoking a cigarette in a long cigarette holder. She was whispering to Hans, who looked wise.

Pierre asked Nella for the next dance and it was Hans' turn to ask Joan. He asked her languidly if she'd mind just sitting and talking, as he hated dancing.

"You seem a sensible girl," he said, looking approvingly at her through his owl-like glasses. "You wouldn't want to drag me into that maelstrom against my will, would you?"

"Oh, no, of course not." Joan was squeezing her hands together nervously. Was it because he didn't think she could dance well that he wanted to sit it out? And what would she say to him? But she need not have worried. He did all the talking. Words came pouring out of him while Joan watched Pierre and Nella dancing together. Nella danced very well. They were doing a tango and the movements suited Nella's slim grace. She was wearing a glittering gown, like a sheath of silver. Joan wondered if Pierre knew Nella very well. Perhaps he liked her better than Joan. Perhaps he wished he had asked Nella to the dance. Joan supposed Nella was an interesting person, the sort of person who has Deep Thoughts.

"Don't you think so?" Hans asked.

"Oh yes," Joan murmured hastily, wondering what Hans had been saying and trying to look as sympathetic as possible.

"It's so nice to talk to someone who really *listens*," said Hans gratefully. Joan felt ashamed of herself.

Pierre and Nella were returning.

"The trouble with the Impressionists is," Pierre was saying, "that they did away with all former standards in art, and we're left with the chaos."

"Ah, yes," said Nella, "but you must remember that chaos can be the beginning of new life. We must start all over again . . . make our own standards."

Joan's heart sank. *She* could not talk like that. She knew

nothing whatever about art. How dull Pierre must think her. No wonder he preferred Nella. She sat silent and miserable, unaware that Gilles was trying to draw her into a conversation.

Why did I come? she thought. Miss Thorpe was right. I don't belong here. I'm only a silly little girl who doesn't know anything.

The orchestra was starting an old-fashioned waltz. Nella was saying some earnest things to Pierre, but Pierre jumped up, turning to Joan.

"Can you dance this?" he asked. And suddenly all Joan's melancholy had vanished. Life was wonderful again.

There were few couples on the floor. Most people found the old-fashioned waltz too hard to do. After a while, only Pierre and Joan were left. The orchestra played on and on. The colored lights whirled and melted around Joan. She felt nothing but Pierre's arm steering her, heard nothing but the music. It was as if she and Pierre were both part of it, in a world of their own—as if they had no bodies any more but were floating off, translated into sound.

They didn't notice that the spotlights had been trained on them and that everyone was looking at them. When they finally stopped there was a thunderous sound of clapping.

Joan felt the hall whirling about her. She looked at Pierre, who smiled down at her. "You can dance . . ." he said, a touch of awe in his voice.

"So can you." Joan smiled back. They returned to their table, feeling as if they had shared a strange and beautiful enchantment.

It was after that dance that Joan found herself *popular.* All sorts of boys came to Pierre and wanted to be intro-duced to her. She was danced off her feet, and Pierre complained he hadn't a chance with her any more. Joan was radiant. She didn't recognize herself. She had always been rather serious, impressed by the duties of life. She'd never known that you could feel as if the air itself were champagne and as if nothing in the world mattered but this blissful moment.

Pierre claimed her for the supper dance, and afterward he took her to the supper room, where a lovely cold buffet was set out on long tables with white cloths on them.

"You're a success," he said, smiling at her. "My friends all want to know who you are, and why they've never met you before."

"Still, I like you best," said Joan, looking at him so affectionately that Pierre blushed.

After supper the dancing went on, but Joan could never remember it very clearly. All the dances seemed to blur together into one great splash of joy and triumph.

Finally it was all over. Joan said good-by to the other members of her group. Gilles and Stella shook her hand cordially, but Nella just reached out her fingertips. Hans lingered over the parting, looking at Joan with a sentimental expression.

"You made a hit there," said Pierre, with an amused smile, as he was driving Joan home.

"With Hans?"

"Yes, he likes you, didn't you notice it?"

"And I didn't even listen to him . . ."

"Nobody listens to Hans," Pierre told her. "But he thinks the world of you. He told me so."

"I can't understand it," said Joan, blushing. "All the other girls were so much cleverer—Nella, now."

"Nella puts on an act," said Pierre. "You're yourself. That's what I like about you."

Joan sat quietly basking in these words of praise till they arrived at Friendly Gables.

"Thank you for a lovely evening, Pierre," she said.

"Thank you for coming," said Pierre. "I loved dancing with you. Perhaps we'll go to a movie sometime, eh?"

"Oh yes, please," said Joan, with shining eyes.

Daddy was waiting up for her, with a cup of coffee. He was pleased that Pierre had brought her home so promptly.

"I like that boy," he said. "And how was the ball?"

"Oh, Daddy, it was *divine!*" And Joan launched into a description of her evening. Patsy heard the noise and came down in kimono and slippers. Daddy raked up the fire and they had a lovely chat, all three of them, Daddy remembering the dances of his youth.

It was quite late when they finally crept up to bed.

TWELVE

A Party for Miss Thorpe

MOTHER was allowed to come down next day for the very first time since the twins had been born. The children wanted to celebrate it. Luckily it was a Saturday. They decorated her chair with pine boughs they had brought in from the garden, and Patsy had baked a special cake, with "**WELCOME MOMMY**" in chocolate letters on the white frosting.

Peter had promised to clean the living room, but his methods were rather cumbersome. He first collected all the furniture into the hall. Then he put all the cleaning

apparatus he could find in the middle of the bare room:
the mops, pail, furniture wax, brooms, vacuum cleaner,
and carpet sweeper. He said that one had to be methodi-
cal. Then he put a disk on the gramophone and worked to
music, which meant that the cleaning was interrupted
every five minutes to change records.

Miss Thorpe finally gave him a helping hand and between the two of them the room looked lovely when
Mother came down. She walked very slowly and came
downstairs one step at a time.

It was just as if a lamp had been lighted, to see her
sitting in her favorite chair again. Joan and Patsy served
tea with their cake. Both of them felt rather heavy-eyed
after their late night. Angela had dressed Timmy, Catherine, and herself in their best clothes. Catherine wore a
huge bow in her hair, of which she was very proud.
Mother commented on her good manners.

"She isn't spilling a crumb," she said, watching Catherine eat her cake.

"Yes, that's because of Miss Thorpe's influenza over
her," explained Timmy. Miss Thorpe beamed with pleasure.

"I must say, Miss Thorpe has done wonders," Mother
declared. "You're all so quiet, and so *clean!*"

"Oh, yes, we have to wash all the time," boasted Timmy.
Somehow it didn't seem terrible any more; he felt proud
of Miss Thorpe. All the children felt proud of her, when
they noticed how pleased Mother was.

"Now we must discuss the christening," said Mother.
"We're having it on the last day Miss Thorpe is here, so
she can be at it too. I want Joan to be Johnny's godmother . . . and I want Patsy to be Jimmy's. She has been
so good, lately, I think she deserves it."

Patsy felt glorified. She'd known that Joan would be godmother to one of the twins but she'd never thought she'd be one herself.

Miss Thorpe was leaving on Wednesday and she was quite sad about it. She said it was the hardest thing about her job that you had to leave people just as you were getting fond of them.

"Come and visit us sometimes," encouraged Mother.

"Yes, I hope to, but it's not the same. I've such lovely friends in England too, whom I won't see for ages. There just isn't *time*."

"Whom did you work for before you came to us?" asked Angela.

"Oh, many people. I looked after an old gentleman in London just before I came over here. He had pneumonia. And he had the sweetest granddaughter—about your age, Patsy. She is studying to be an actress. A beautiful child, lovely red hair and deep blue eyes. They say she has lots of talent. I was very sorry to leave her, she was so grateful for a little mothering. She lost her own mother in the war."

"What was her name?" asked Patsy, who had listened with a queer sense of recognition.

"Eunice, Eunice Spencer."

"Our Una!" cried Joan, Patsy, and Peter. Mother too was amazed that Miss Thorpe should know those dear old friends. Miss Thorpe had to tell everything she knew about them: what their flat was like, and how Eunice kept house for her grandfather and attended dramatic school three times a week.

"Does Eunice go to dances?" asked Joan. But Miss Thorpe told her that in England girls that young don't go to dances yet.

"And is Mr. Spencer all right again?" asked Mother.

Miss Thorpe assured her that he had got over his pneumonia beautifully.

Mother couldn't stay downstairs for long. She still got tired very easily. But before she went up to her room again the children had an official announcement to make.

"You and Miss Thorpe are invited to a party tomorrow, at a Secret Place," they said, and enjoyed Miss Thorpe's mystified expression.

In a way it was sad, having to give up their secret.

"But it doesn't matter," said Patsy "because we like Homework anyway, secret or no secret."

"And you never know, it may come in handy in the future," said Peter. "There might be other people we won't like." Which made them all laugh.

They had been preparing for this party for several days. It would be Miss Thorpe's good-by party. Timmy's money was to be spent on refreshments.

"We must have tea," decided Patsy. "Not the bags, but loose tea."

"And marmalade," said Timmy.

"No, silly, that's only for breakfast. Miss Thorpe likes plain biscuits. Nothing fancy," said Peter.

"But she loves flowers," Joan remembered.

Mother had to help, because a dollar wasn't enough. She said it was all right to buy a tin of English biscuits out of the housekeeping money, so they spent Timmy's dollar on flowers. They bought them on Saturday and took them straight up to Homework. There was a momentary scare, when they bumped into Miss Thorpe on the stairs, but luckily the flowers were wrapped up.

"I think she noticed something, though," said Peter afterward. "She gave us such a queer look."

"Well, you looked so guilty," remarked Angela.

That Saturday night the children slept fitfully, disturbed by dreams in which Miss Thorpe figured in a dual capacity. One moment she would be a terrifying specter, and then again she was all goodness. Peter had an especially frightening dream in which he conducted a mild and pleasant Miss Thorpe to their sanctuary, only to see her turn into a witch and start smashing everything. Patsy, on the other hand, dreamed that they were cowering in their shelter, they heard Miss Thorpe's steps on the ladder, they were petrified, clutching one another—and then they heard a kind voice and Miss Thorpe came in, smiling and distributing biscuits.

They had to wait for the party till after lunch on Sunday, as the morning was filled with church-going and cooking the dinner. But at last the great moment arrived. Miss Thorpe was blindfolded before she was led up the ladder to the attic. She said she couldn't *imagine* what was going to happen! Mother climbed up very slowly, with Daddy's help, and Peter gave her a hand from above to steady her as she stepped off the ladder. The closet door was propped open so the twins could be heard if they woke up and cried.

The children had cleaned their den extra well, knowing Miss Thorpe's horror of dirt. When the blindfold was taken off Miss Thorpe was really amazed. She had no idea they had made such a lovely hut.

"So that's where you were, all the time!" she exclaimed.

"And you never guessed, did you?" crowed Timmy.

"Well, I realized you were *somewhere*," said Miss Thorpe with a little smile. "And I did guess it was up in the attic. Sometimes you forgot and made a noise, you know! I would have come up to investigate, but your mother

didn't seem worried about it and didn't encourage me."
She smiled again. "Still, I'd *no* idea it was a lovely place
like this." She was truly impressed.

"You have very creative children," she told Mother.
Mother tried to look modest.

Catherine too was impressed. She ran around rapturously, investigating everything. She discovered Caramel
and Custard, who had been kept in the attic, out of reach
of her lethal affection. She pounced on them.

There was a table full of delicious surprises. Tea and
English biscuits for the grownups and ice cream and cupcakes for the children—that was Daddy's contribution.

And then the children announced that they had a little
act they wanted to do for Miss Thorpe. They retired
behind a curtain, where they had rigged up a sort of stage.
The grownups drank their tea and chatted while a lot of
giggling went on behind the curtain. Finally it was pulled
aside, revealing an enormous cardboard shoe in profile,
cleverly constructed and realistically painted, with windows cut in it through which peeped the faces of Timmy,
Angela, and Peter. Joan came hobbling out with a shawl
around her, leaning on a stick and moaning. Behind the
shoe the children were screaming and banging on pots.
Then Patsy came on the stage dressed as a nurse and
holding a large safety pin and a box of baby powder. She
went to the old woman, took her pulse, made her stick
out her tongue, and fed her some medicine, but the old
woman kept moaning, holding her head and pointing
behind her, where the children were making more noise.

The nurse took a broom and went behind the shoe,
chased away the children, and came back with a plate full
of sandwiches.

Meanwhile Peter was reciting.

"There was an old woman who lived in a shoe
She had so many children she didn't know what to do.
So she called for Miss Thorpe, who brought powder
      and pins,
And went to the cradle to settle the twins.

"She took up a broom and she swept all the floors
And she chased off the children to play out of doors,
Then she fixed up a meal with tea, toast, and jam
And the little old woman said, 'How happy I am!' "

Then Peter said, "Three cheers for Miss Thorpe!" and the old woman, and the nurse, and the children all cheered so hard that the shoe tumbled down and buried them and they had to crawl out again with shrieks and giggles.

Mother and Daddy applauded hard, Catherine was squealing with laughter, but Miss Thorpe sat very still, as if she didn't know whether to laugh or to cry.

"We have a gift for you," announced Angela. "Because you have taken such good care of us. We made it ourselves. Joan did most, but we all helped." She handed Miss Thorpe a tissue-wrapped parcel tied with blue ribbon. Miss Thorpe opened it tremulously and found a lovely white apron with big pockets. In the pockets were safety pins, bandage rolls, measuring tape, scissors, a needlecase, bobby pins, and all those little items that are so useful to have and yet seem too trivial to buy. Miss Thorpe looked at it with trembling lips.

"Don't you like it?" asked Timmy.

"Yes, dear, I do," said Miss Thorpe, blowing her nose hard.

"We wanted to *please* you—" Timmy pointed out relentlessly.

"Oh, you have, you *have!*" said Miss Thorpe, and to his

disgust she kissed him. But he remembered that it was her party, so he didn't protest.

Poor Catherine had been rather left out, so Joan let her give the bunch of daffodils to Miss Thorpe. Catherine hadn't really understood that Miss Thorpe was going. She realized it only because of the party. Suddenly she threw herself against Miss Thorpe's knees, clasping them, and wailing in a heart-rending voice, "Don't go! Don't go!" This completely finished what was left of that poor lady and made the children wonder afterward whether the party had been a success. But Mother assured them it had.

And so the day of the christening arrived. The ceremony would be at four o'clock and the children were to come to the church after school. Mother had invited Uncle Armand, Paul, and Paul's father, and afterward they were to have tea at Friendly Gables.

"We'll have to be in our school uniforms, Mommy," said Joan. "Does that matter?"

"No, dear, as long as you're clean," said Mother. "Take a comb with you to tidy your hair. The babies have to look well, of course. It's *such* a pity we only have one long christening robe."

But Miss Thorpe had a surprise for them. On Wednesday morning she came down with a blue paper parcel, tied with white ribbon. She gave it to Mother at breakfast, when Daddy and all the children sat around the table, basking in Mother's presence.

"This is my farewell gift," she said. And when Mother opened it she found a lovely long christening robe, a perfect match for the other, except that it didn't have such expensive lace. Miss Thorpe had bought the material on the Saturday the children had been away—and had worked at it secretly ever since. It was all stitched by hand.

"Oh, Miss Thorpe," said Mother, deeply touched, "you shouldn't have done it!" But she had tears of joy in her eyes. Now she would not have to discriminate against one of her precious sons.

"Do you think I could bear for one of my babies to be less beautiful than the other?" said Miss Thorpe defiantly.

It was a proud moment for Joan and Patsy when each held a beautifully gowned three-and-a-half-weeks'-old brother in her arms at the baptismal font. Joan had begged for Jimmy, he was her favorite, and Patsy had Johnny instead. He was more serious than Jimmy but had a very gentle look.

The guests were all grouped around as Monsieur le Curé poured water on the two little heads and solemnly baptized them James Michael and John William.

Mother had tears in her eyes. It was part of the joy of giving birth, to bring her babies back to God afterward. Daddy shared her feelings. He had put his arm through hers and she leaned against him.

Miss Thorpe felt proud and sad. She knew she had done a good job, looking after the Mitchells, but she was very sorry to leave them. As she watched the faces of the six older children, so earnestly intent on the ceremony, she could not understand why she had thought them all so tiresome at first.

Uncle Armand's eyes were twinkling. After animals, he loved babies best. Paul and his stepfather exchanged glances; a warm friendship was developing between those two.

Joan looked down on the little red face of Jimmy, and dreamed of having a home of her own one day, but Patsy's thoughts were all with Johnny and her duties as a godmother. She promised in her heart to watch over this new little brother of hers.

Peter's glance slid now and again toward Paul. He felt pleased that all was right with him and that they were friends now.

Angela dreamily watched the beauty of the stained-glass windows and the way the sun shone through them, while Timmy looked at the twins, to see if baptism had changed them. Only Catherine felt unhappy. Why were all these lovely things being done to the twins, and not to her?

She brooded about it afterward, when they had left the cool darkness of the church and walked into the sparkling April sunshine.

"Why were the twins blessed, and not me?" she asked.

"You've been 'blessed' too, dear," Mother answered her with a smile.

"But I don't *feel* blessed," complained Catherine.

At home a beautiful christening cake waited for them, a surprise from Daddy. It had two storks on it, each with a sugar baby in its beak.

The real babies were on display in the living room, lying side by side on the sofa, their long robes spread out. You could already see the difference in character between them. Johnny hadn't cried at all when he was baptized and now lay staring peacefully, with quiet, absorbed eyes. Jimmy had roared vigorously as soon as he had felt the water, and now he was peering about curiously, responding with smiles and grimaces to the admiration lavished on him.

Joan said she thought Jimmy was the more intelligent one. Patsy defended her Johnny by saying he had thoughts inside himself that interested him more than what happened outside. And anyway, when he did smile, he looked much sweeter. Joan conceded that he might be the more loving one.

"Have you realized," said Peter, "that the twins are Canadians?"

The Mitchells hadn't thought of that yet. "Imagine having two nationalities in our family!" they exclaimed. "I wonder, will we notice the difference?"

Peter said to Paul, "You've become partly American, and we've become partly Canadian." Paul nodded. He kept looking at the babies; he loved them.

Joan was serving the tea, and Peter and Patsy went around offering slices of cake. Monsieur le Curé had been invited too, of course, and stood talking with Daddy. He accepted a piece of the christening cake, and was biting into it when he saw two dark eyes looking at him with a shocked expression. They belonged to Catherine, who pulled Patsy's sleeve and asked in a loud whisper, "Is he a priest?"

"Yes, dear," Patsy whispered back.

"No!" protested Catherine in a scandalized voice. "He is just a *man*, he *eats!*"

Monsieur le Curé chuckled and stored the incident away among the anecdotes he liked to tell at dull social occasions.

Uncle Armand was talking to Mother about his nephew. "It was your children that got 'im out of 'is bad mood. Paul 'ad never seen a large, 'appy family. It was a great lesson to 'im. 'E was spoiled. 'E needed brothers and sisters. And I've 'eard," he said lowering his voice, "that 'e will get a little brother or sister in the fall."

"Oh, I'm so glad," exclaimed Mother. "That will be the making of him. Is he going back to Boston with his new father?"

"Oh yes, and Paul is 'appy about it. Ted Morrison is a wealthy man. Paul will 'ave a good life, of a certainty."

The Mitchell children had made friends with Mr. Morrison, whose broad genial features beamed good nature. Paul was proud that they liked him. He wanted to show his stepfather the attic, so the children all trooped up there, Catherine tagging after them, anxious to play with the kitten.

Mr. Morrison greatly admired the den. "We must build you one *just* like that at home," he told Paul.

The Mitchell children didn't say anything but they thought the more. As if you could duplicate their Homework!

The guests were all leaving. Mr. Morrison asked the Mitchells to come and visit his home in Boston. "You'll all be welcome," he said with a wide sweep of his hand which took in even the babies. He offered to take Monsieur le Curé home, so the priest got into Mr. Morrison's car, where Uncle Armand and Paul were already seated.

Afterward Miss Thorpe left too. Peter carried her suitcases to the taxi for her. Miss Thorpe kissed everyone except Daddy. She and Mother both wept a little, and Mother thanked her for the wonderful care she had taken of her family.

"Not at all, not at all." Miss Thorpe sniffed, her nose pink again.

They all waved from the doorway until the taxi had gone around the corner. Then a stillness descended on the Mitchell home, broken only by the wailing of a twin, whom Joan hushed. The family settled around the fire for a chat before Mother went up to bed. She was tired but happy as she leaned back in her own chair. Daddy sat in his, opposite her, stretching his legs with a grunt of contentment. The children dropped down on the hearth rug and on footstools.

"It's really only been a little over three weeks," said Peter thoughtfully, "but it seemed *ages.*"

"Yes, it did, didn't it?" agreed Daddy.

"And now we're all by ourselves again," sighed Patsy. "Isn't it lovely? Just *us.*"

"Yes," whispered Angela in an awed voice, "all *ten* of us."

About the Author

Hilda van Stockum was born in Rotterdam, Holland, in 1908, daughter of a Dutch naval officer and an Irish-Dutch mother from whom she early learned English. Story-telling, art, fun and home-schooling (until age 10) enriched her young days. Her first plan was to become an artist. At age 16, having moved to Ireland with her family, she attended the School of Art in Dublin; later, the Dutch Academy in Amsterdam. Writing frequent letters to her mother (between Ireland and Holland), she developed her descriptive skills which would blossom into a career of distinction, writing and illustrating children's books.

Those books began immediately after her marriage to an American, Ervin Marlin, in 1932, and continued over a 43-year period to roll from her pen. *A Day on Skates*, set in Holland, helped pay her way to America. Other early books captured life in Ireland. But soon the years of marriage and motherhood to six young Marlins offered a fresh field for good story and good humor. *The Mitchells: Five for Victory* draws directly from her family life with growing children, as do its sequels, *Canadian Summer* and *Friendly Gables*. Empathy with children and an instinct for the importance of small things characterize these and all Miss van Stockum's works. As her children grew up, Miss van Stockum took inspiration from other sources, returning, in some tales, both to Holland and Ireland and venturing even to Africa. The Marlins settled eventually in England to be near three daughters and numerous grandchildren. Today, Mrs. Marlin (Hilda van Stockum) continues to wield a paintbrush that fully justifies the renown she earned in her *other* career as artist.

The Mitchells: Five for Victory
by Hilda van Stockum

Daddy's off to war. The rest of the Mitchell family are left to hold the fort in their Washington D.C. home. One of Daddy's last admonitions is to his oldest daughter Joan— "No Dogs!" Joan, who would dearly love to have such a pet, puts her energies instead into forming a club to help at home. However, as one unexpected pet after another joins the "Mitchell Zoo," Joan wonders what her father will have to say about it all. Warm new friendships and a few awkward situations result from the children's zeal to help out their mother on the homefront. Amid the busy whirlwind of this lively family there are also moments of sadness, of fear and of unlooked-for joy. No life can be quite normal during times of war. Join conscientious Joan, soft-hearted Patsy, steady Peter, unpredictable Angela and adventurous baby Timmy in a unique, often hilarious story of family life.

Canadian Summer
by Hilda van Stockum

The Mitchells are leaving Washington D. C. The war is over and Daddy's work is moving the family—expanded now to include baby Catherine—to Canada. However, he hasn't been able to find a decent house in Montreal. Mother and Grannie arrive with the children to find that the only available housing is a remote summer cottage. What more could six healthy children want beyond a lake and a forest and a little camping? What less could Mother and Grannie wish than a primitive, isolated cabin from which to keep track of six city children? And Daddy comes home only on the weekends! Needless to say, an unforgettable summer unfolds for the Mitchell clan.